ALIEN INVASION
and Other Inconveniences

ALIEN INVASION
and Other Inconveniences

BRIAN YANSKY

CANDLEWICK PRESS

Copyright © 2010 by Brian Yansky

First edition 2010

Library of Congress Cataloging-in-Publication Data
Yansky, Brian.
Alien invasion and other inconveniences / Brian Yansky.
— 1st U.S. ed.
p. cm.
Summary: When a race of aliens quietly takes over the earth, high schooler Jesse finds himself a slave to an inept alien leader — a situation that brightens as Jesse develops telepathic powers and attracts the attention of two beautiful girls.
ISBN 978-0-7636-4384-3
[1. Extraterrestrial beings — Fiction. 2. Telepathy — Fiction.
3. Science fiction.] I. Title.
PZ7.Y19536Re 2010
[Fic] — dc22   2009049103

10 11 12 13 14 15 16 RRC 10 9 8 7 6 5 4 3 2 1

Printed in Crawfordsville, IN, U.S.A.

This book was typeset in Mendoza.

Candlewick Press
99 Dover Street
Somerville, Massachusetts 02144

visit us at www.candlewick.com

For my wife, Frances

(((((1)))))

It takes less time for them to conquer the world than it takes me to brush my teeth. That's pretty disappointing.

I'm in history class, listening to Mr. Whitehead's description of the Great Depression. "Everything was changed," he says, tapping his desk with two fingers the way he does when he wants to call attention to something he's said. I know he's about to repeat himself because he always does after the finger tap. I turn to Jackson to mouth the sentence as Mr. Whitehead speaks it, which is something we do to combat the big-yawn boredom.

But the second sentence never comes from Mr. Whitehead. It doesn't come from Jackson or me, either. Instead a voice comes into my head. THAT'S RIGHT.

A VOICE. NOT MINE. IN MY HEAD. The voice says, *You are one of the few product who can hear. Congratulations. Stand by for a message.*

Stand by for a message sounds like some kind of public-service announcement, so naturally I'm thinking I'm crazy. I'm imagining I'm bound for a room with locks on the outside and keepers in white coats asking me questions along the lines of "Would you like another cookie?"

But there really is a message. It comes a second later.

I am Lord Vertenomous and I claim this planet in the name of the Republic of Sanginia. You have been conquered by the greatest beings in the known universe. It took ten seconds.

The world is conquered in ten seconds? Come on. Also, the voice itself isn't particularly scary. Not like the breathy, booming voice of, say, Darth Vader. It's more of a whisper and a little squeaky around the edges. In fact, I'm kind of disappointed that the imagination of my damaged mind couldn't do better. But then I notice what I've been too freaked to notice before. No one is moving. Every single person, including Mr. Whitehead, looks sound asleep. I feel a shadow over me then, and it practically knocks me off my feet. I struggle to breathe. I force deep breaths. Then I do what you do when people are sleeping at a totally inappropriate time and in a totally inappropriate place. I try to wake them. I shake Carlee Thorton, who is the best student in school and would never, ever fall asleep in class. I punch Jackson on the arm.

"Jackson, dude, it's me, Jesse. Wake up," I plead. He doesn't.

I don't know it then, but this is what happens to most of the Earth's population. They go to sleep. They never wake up.

I try my cell but it's dead. I go out into the hall and try some good old-fashioned screaming. No one screams back.

I'm all alone.

It's so quiet.

The alien voice comes back. My body jerks as if a cold hand has grabbed me from behind, and my heart, which definitely wasn't doing a slow jog before, sprints. The voice says, *It should be clear that you are weak and we are strong. You are now our slave, unless you are unable to be a slave, in which case you are dead. We are sorry for your loss. This is a most excellent planet. Lovely blue sky. Most excellent green vegetation. We are going to like it here. Thank you for not completely destroying it.*

I do what a lot of people (I find out later) who remain awake do. I run. I run toward home.

I get only a few feet beyond the school doors before the truth of the alien's claims hits me. I have to stop.

I heave my breakfast right there on the sidewalk. Cars are crashed all over the place. Bodies fallen everywhere: people, birds, squirrels, dogs, and cats. I step over and around the bodies. So many of them. But the strange thing is that most people look like they're asleep. It looks like they just got very tired all at once and lay down for a nap.

"Anybody?" I shout as I start to run. "Anybody here?"

But nobody is. People are all over the place, but they aren't here. Nothing is. No sounds at all. I even think for a second that maybe I've lost my hearing, but I can hear my own short, sharp breaths.

I don't make it home. I make it about two blocks before the Sanginians stop me. In the same way the alien voice didn't inspire terror, the aliens don't look particularly frightening. They're not giant roaches or hooded, hollow-eyed ghoul types or even some version of the biggest-foreheads-in-the-universe Klingons. They're small. I'm just six feet and I tower over them. They appear to be hairless. Their eyes are large and round, almost cartoonish. Their skin has a slight green tint to it. I suppose maybe they could be from some remote tribe in the Amazon, the kind you'd see on a National Geographic special or something. If you had to sum them up with a quick description, you'd say "little green men."

They ask me to please come with them. I'm a wrestler and I have a black belt in tae kwon do, and my father was in the Special Forces and taught me a lot of moves. I try to punch one and kick the other, but I can't do either. They stop me without so much as moving a finger. I'm screaming in pain; I drop helplessly to my knees.

Please come with us, one of them says. This time I notice that his mouth doesn't move.

I get up, but my mind is filled with a thick fog. Everything is distant and unclear. I join a group of people; they herd us to downtown Houston. I step over and around bodies all the way. It's like being in a nightmare, like I'm not really all there. Large ships land everywhere. They pick up bodies with some kind of device that sucks them up into the ships. They're like gigantic, sucking garbage-truck ships and we're the garbage. I want to scream, but I can't. I'm ashamed and I'm helpless.

I'm put in this big room in a building. There are alien guards all around. Once we're inside, I slowly begin to feel more like myself. I'm able to move again on my own, able to form thoughts that feel like mine. I think, *Where are my parents? Are they alive? Is anyone I love, like, or even know alive?*

I look around. Most people look the way I feel: dazed and exhausted. A woman in the corner is crying.

A man keeps pulling a quarter out of his pocket and putting it back in and pulling it out again. A couple starts arguing, shouting at each other. One of the aliens tells them to stop, but they don't listen. You can tell they are the kind of people who have lived their lives not listening. The alien does something, and they drop. It's like they've been shot through the heart.

"I'm sorry for your loss," the alien says to the dead bodies like you'd say "Excuse me" to someone you bumped into passing down a hall. One thing you have to say about these aliens is they're very polite. They are probably the most polite killers around. My mother is big on manners, and I can't help thinking she'd approve, except for the killing part of course.

We spend the night in the building, which I realize is a bank. It has teller windows and a vault and all. I could probably go help myself to as much money as I want. The aliens wouldn't care. The money is as worthless as dirt to them. I guess it's as worthless as dirt to us now, too.

The next morning they assign us to numbered groups. I'm in a group assigned to work downtown. They tell us we are slaves now, what they call *product,* and that eventually we will have private masters. For now we're the property of the Republic of Sanginia, the greatest republic in the known universe. They think a lot of themselves. They're the greatest beings from the greatest republic. What are we? We're nothing.

Houston is like a ghost town. A few days later, I'm taken to Austin, and it's like a ghost town there, too. I guess it's like a ghost planet. No buildings have been destroyed, no houses. At first glance the world doesn't look all that different. But it feels different. It feels empty. It sounds empty, too. It's so quiet. More than anything, the silence makes me feel what I've lost. The Earth is no longer ours.

««««(2)»»»»

There are thirty-one people on our crew. Twenty guys and eleven girls. I've asked around. The oldest person here is forty and the youngest is thirteen. Most are in their teens and twenties. It was the same way at the bank. Apparently, a couple of people on the crew saw kids survive, but there aren't any kids here and there weren't any at the bank. Where are they?

The crew I'm working on and several other crews are assigned to the task of gathering machines. We gather them from offices and condos. Anywhere there's a machine, we find it. When we do, we take it to places the aliens have set up to destroy the machines. I'm talking about cars, computers, phones, toasters, microwaves, even televisions. The aliens really seem to enjoy destroying them. What could an alien have against TV? This is another alien behavior my mom would approve of. She thought TV lowered everyone's IQ every time they watched it.

About two weeks later, after a long morning of collecting machines, a bus pulls up. The Sanginian who's been ordering us around all day orders me and this guy named Michael to get in.

You're being transferred to Lord Vertenomous's house. Congratulations.

"Why congratulations?" I ask.

They don't like questions. And they're not big on answers. Mostly they just look at us with those big creepy eyes. But the boss Sanginian surprises me and answers. *Because you are superior product.*

"Like a good pair of shoes?" I say.

He stares at me with those big creepy eyes and then turns away. One answer is all I get.

Michael and I take the last two seats at the back of the bus. I think he's a little older than I am, but I don't know much about him. I've heard he was a big-time football player in Florida. He looks like an athlete. He also looks like someone who thinks a lot of himself.

We're going down streets we haven't gone down before. We pass other crews loading machines into the alien transport ships.

"How's it feel?" Michael says. First words he's ever said to me.

"What?"

"Being a slave."

"It's great," I say. "How about you?"

He wants attitude, I'll give him attitude. When the situation calls for it, I am an excellent attitude giver.

"It's in my genes, right?" he says. "I should be real good at it."

He smiles at me, but it isn't a real smile. His jaw clenches, and his eyes get small and hard, and I can see how much he'd like to hit something—me, he thinks, but really just something.

"Right," I say, trying to be sarcastic.

I get the feeling Michael wants an apology from me, which I don't understand exactly.

"You think that's right?"

"You ever heard of the word *sarcasm*?"

Michael is trying to stare me down. I pretend I don't notice. He looks away, out the window. "I was going to be a star. I was going to have whatever I wanted. Everyone said so. Pro football star. I wasn't a jerk about it, either. Not me. I was humble. What an idiot."

"Why an idiot?" I say, curious in spite of myself.

"I should have been grabbing everything I could."

Even though I don't like the guy's attitude and am not especially fond of football stars and egomaniacs in general, I know what he means. What did I miss by not grabbing everything I could? And now it's gone. Everything's gone.

"I can see that," I say.

"You can't see anything. You aren't me."

Again, the attitude. Does he really think he's the only one who's lost anything, everything?

Michael bangs the seat in front of him with an open hand. "Now here I am two hundred years ago. Somebody's property."

"We both are."

"Don't give me that *both* stuff. You don't know. It isn't in you like it's in me."

I feel the need to point out the obvious. "You haven't been a slave."

"I've got the memory in me, and I can't get rid of it. You know how I know this is true? I always thought something was gonna come and take everything away from me. I always thought that. My mother and my sisters told me I was crazy, but here we are."

"You always thought that?"

"That's right. I knew something like this was gonna happen."

"Like little green men from outer space were going to invade Earth and ruin your football career? You knew that?"

He glares at me. I glare back. Then, I don't know why exactly, but we both kind of smile. And once we smile, we start laughing. I can't even say what's so funny, but I can't stop laughing. People on the bus turn around and look at us like we're crazy. I realize then I haven't heard laughter in what seems like an eternity.

When Michael stops, he says, "Okay, Tex. Maybe you got me there."

We arrive at the great lord's house, which is more like a palace. Someone has chopped off the top of a hill to build it. A stone wall, like the wall of a castle, surrounds it. The grounds are lush, with plants and trees. Fountains and pools are linked by a stream that gurgles and twists its way through the grounds. Whoever owned this before the alien invasion must have been a bazillionaire. He must have had so much money he could do anything he wanted. But it didn't do him any good when the aliens came. If he's alive, he's just like the rest of us now. Product.

Two other buses are unloading in the large brick parking area. It's like before. Most of the people are young, with a few older people and no kids. I notice a girl who looks a little like Paris Hilton. I see that Michael notices her, too.

Six Handlers are in the parking area to watch us. I've only seen one Handler before, but they're easy to spot. They're warriors. They're a little bigger than the other Sanginians, and they carry themselves like my dad and his friends, like soldiers.

One of the Handlers herds us inside. It's like he's all around us, like he's able to multiply himself so there are suddenly thirty or forty of him. He tells us, in our minds, that we are superior product and have been chosen to work in the House of Lord Vertenomous, the leader of the invasion and First Citizen of the colony.

If he expects me to be impressed or thankful, he can forget it. But he doesn't seem to expect anything— unless you count total obedience. He's pretty clear about that. *I expect total obedience. If I do not get that from you, then you can expect total death. I will be sorry for your loss.*

Boys go to the second floor and girls to the third. Five or six to a room. We're going to have to sleep on the floor, but at least they put out pillows and blankets and sheets. Michael and I make up places over by a window.

"Aren't we lucky to be superior product?" I say. "We get to be Lord Vert's slaves."

"Lord Vert?" Michael says. Then nods and smiles. "Yeah, okay, Lord Vert."

"Lord Vert, big-time First Citizen of the Sans."

"We're probably never going to leave here," Michael says, looking out the window.

"Don't say that," I say. "Just don't. *Sexual intercourse.* I hate the *illegitimate sons* so much."

Michael doesn't know me all that well, but he's giving me the look I get a lot from my friends. I mean *got* a lot. One they especially gave me when I invented alternatives to swearing.

"It's my mom," I tell him. "She was an English teacher. She said swearing was just a form of laziness, so she convinced my dad and me to come up with alternatives. It was kind of like a game. I got in the habit of it. Once at a wrestling match I called my opponent a son of a female dog and a fatherless biped. The guy was so confused, I got a two-point takedown."

Michael shakes his head. "Dude, I've known people who pretend to be crazy, but you, my friend, are the real deal."

Sure, I hear the rest of it, but what I hear loudest is "my friend" and somehow, in spite of everything, this makes me feel a little better.

(((((3)))))

LORD VERTENOMOUS

My dearest,

We are making progress, but it is slow. Everything must be done or redone. No communication tunnels, no flight paths. The land here is unattractively hilly, and the buildings too tall; even the furniture is ridiculously large and cumbersome. But the most troubling aspect of this world is the clutter of machines. It is uncomfortable to be in proximity to so many of them, though they are primitive and harmless to us. The product even used them to travel down paved paths on the surface—big hunks of metal hurtling down narrow concrete paths. Absurd and an abomination to the natural green of the world. They have destroyed so much with their brutal and mis-guided attempts to civilize. Naturally, one can see how a species such as this, destructive and self-destructive by nature, would eventu-ally have been conquered by their machines as so many other civilizations in the universe have. Our arrival is fortuitous.

The scouts' assessments of the species is accurate, but surprisingly, a few of them can hear if we create a link. This will add to overall product value. We have lost more of them than anticipated in the process of learning how to avoid harming them. Those who cannot hear are quite fragile in the way of some primitives, and we've often killed when we meant only to punish. However, due to their size, I believe they will make excellent slaves on planets in need of physical labor. I should prepare you and the girls for that. They are extremely ugly. Not only are they grossly large, but they have no green or blue in their skin. Also they have tiny, beady eyes, strangely shaped small heads, and, I'm sorry to say, hair. Nevertheless, the world itself is quite beautiful. Green everywhere. The sky is often astonishingly blue.

I am eagerly anticipating your arrival and the arrival of the girls and, of course, the colonists. I have a house. Although I'm sure you will find much lacking, it will, I think, suffice until materials to build a real home arrive.

)))) (4)))))

In the morning the aliens wake us with an obnoxious *Wake, product* followed by a faint shock. I actually miss being woken by my mom. She had a morning person's enthusiasm that was as irritating as a pep squad, but I miss it now.

They order us to gather by the big pool. I get there early, and only one other person is there; a pretty girl. She has pale skin and long, curly black hair and wears glasses that don't hide her dark eyes or the fact that tears are coming out of them.

"Are you okay?" I realize it's a dumb question right after I ask it. Who's okay?

"No," she says.

I try to be more specific. "What's wrong?"

"I just saw them kill a girl. She lost it—started screaming. One of them told her to stop, and when she didn't, the alien turned her off. That's what it was like. It was like the alien flipped a switch, and the girl dropped to the floor dead."

She's looking at me like she hopes I can say something that will make things less terrible. I've got nothing.

"I'm sorry," I say finally, just to break the silence because it feels like it's trying to break us.

She shivers. "We aren't anything. They're right, in a way. They can do whatever they want to us, kill us even, and we can't do a thing about it."

"Don't say we aren't anything."

I know how she feels. They're so strong and we're so weak. Sometimes I've felt so weak I think I'll solve the problem of my weakness by not existing at all. Three people used that solution during the short time I worked on the crew downtown.

I look into those pretty dark eyes. I feel her sadness and my own like something trying to pull us under, and I get mad. They've taken everything, but they won't take this. I won't let them. "We matter."

"Why? Why do we matter?"

"We're the last people," I say.

Then she does something surprising. She leans over and kisses me on the cheek. Her lips are soft. Her hair brushes against the side of my face. The kiss itself lasts about a second, but I feel it long after.

Others are around us by then. A few stragglers are still coming out of the house. The aliens order us to form lines. They give us assignments. I'm outside. The girl is in. She smiles at me before she goes into the house. It's a sad smile but a smile just the same.

(((((5)))))

LORD VERTENOMOUS

To Senator & High Lord Vertenomous:

Our scouts were largely correct in their assessment of this planet. They are as primitive as we thought, although it seems that several thousand are capable of hearing. The extent of machine use was underestimated, which I think you might include in your own reports to the president and High Council.

We have destroyed more product than I'd hoped. They are a willful species, and this has made them difficult to categorize, assign, and control. They will learn.

The colony is secure for development. There are remote regions where some product may still remain loose (we have initiated sweeps, so I am certain most of the free product has been exterminated). However, those that remain are not a threat.

My report, of course, goes into great detail on all these subjects as well as on plans for development. Right now our biggest challenge is destroying the machines and removing some of the products' primitive structures. This will take time, but I expect more design and reconstruction crews to arrive before one more revolution of their moon. Given the quantity of product and the quality of the environment, I am certain the company will have no trouble attracting settlers. This will be a desirable and profitable colony. Congratulations.

ATTACHED NOTE TO THE OFFICIAL CORRESPONDENCE:

Dear Father,

If you could expedite my wife and daughters' arrival, I would be very grateful. This is an excellent planet, but it is difficult to be so far away from civilization and my family. There is something in the primary species here that troubles me—some melancholy aspect maybe.

Sometimes their minds become shadowy and difficult to read, and at other times there are disturbing spikes of raw power that must be some kind of feedback from our minds. It would be a great comfort to have my family here as I build this colony.

I hope all goes well on Sanginia.

There are probably about sixty of us living at Lord Vert's, but sometimes they bus in workers who can't "hear." We at Lord Vert's are all hearing product. That's what they call those of us with enough tele- pathic ability that they can speak to us in our minds. Because of this talent (or is it a curse?), they some- times bus us to other work sites to use us as trans- lators for nonhearing slaves. This allows the aliens to avoid talking, which they hate to do. Their voices creak like rusty door hinges. I think it actually hurts them to talk.

This morning, there isn't a cloud in the sky. We walk across the lawn, still damp with dew. The Sans have us building four separate dorms, so they break us up into four crews. Michael and I are on the same crew. We're assigned to the dorm that is closest to being finished.

"Do you think they think we all look alike?" I ask him as we enter the dorm.

"Shut up," he says.

He says this to me pretty often. I don't take offense because I've gotten used to it. In fact I've come to view it as a sign of affection, though I keep this observation to myself.

"I'm just saying, they all sort of look alike to me," I say.

"They're all the same color," he says.

"Yeah, so?"

"So, we aren't."

"Maybe they don't notice."

"Shut up," he says.

A Handler orders us to paint the main room. We slip into jumpsuits that I think are supposed to be for mechanics. Before we arrived, the aliens had filled a room with clothes for us. It looked like a mix of Gap, Old Navy, and stuff from expensive stores. We got the jumpsuits the day we started painting.

We paint with this guy in his thirties named Jerome. He's a black guy, thin and ropy and talkative. Well, more than talkative. His mouth does not stop moving; it's kind of hard to figure out how he breathes with all those words tumbling out all the time. He's got a GAY PRIDE button on his shirt. It's strange. How can it matter now? Somehow it does to Jerome, though, and I like that it does. Michael doesn't. He doesn't like anything about Jerome.

Jerome's painting ability isn't even close to his talking ability. He's messy and slow. He spends probably an hour on the subject of his coming out of the closet and how it took him so long to come out because he was repressed by his father, a homophobic Florida redneck.

"Finally, last month I proclaimed myself gay and what happens? Alien invasion. Can you believe it?"

"Sometimes yes and sometimes no," I say.

He nods enthusiastically. He points at me with his little-used paintbrush. "Yeah, you one of them deep thinkers, ain't you?"

Michael makes a totally uncalled-for snort. Then he adds, "Jesus," in case we somehow missed the totally unsubtle meaning of that snort.

The room we're painting is big. We're painting it green. The Sans love green. It's like some alien obsession. The whole world will be green if they have their way, and I guess they will.

Michael is keeping his back to Jerome as much as possible, and finally Jerome says, "Brother don't like gays."

"I don't like people who never shut up," Michael says.

"Just might be I got something you want to hear, sweets."

"Don't call me that." He stops painting. His back isn't to Jerome now.

"Oh, Lord. We've been invaded. We've lost everything. We're slaves, for God's sake, and the brother is worried about being called sweets. Unbelievable."

"Didn't say I was worried. Just said don't call me that."

Jerome is taller than Michael, and something about the way he stands makes me think that he knows things about fighting. Then it's more than just a thought. *I feel like I'm not entirely myself. I'm in a bar and some guy calls me a queer and I whisper to the guy that he's queer too but doesn't know it. The guy's like a bear. Huge. I think I'm about to get killed. The guy takes a swing and I step back. Then I realize it's not me. It's Jerome. We knee the guy in the groin, and then when he doubles over, we knee him twice to the chin and down the guy goes. We step back and roundhouse-kick the guy in the head.* That's it. I'm back to myself. I'm confused. It takes me a few seconds to work it out. I saw a memory, Jerome's memory.

Besides the fact that I now *know* Jerome could kick

Michael's ass, any fighting draws the aliens' attention. They tend to punish us quickly and severely for behavior they don't like.

I say, "What do you want to tell us, Jerome?"

Jerome turns to look at me. It could go either way. He's mad; Michael's mad. He shakes his head. "Looks like you're the only one's got any sense here. I seen someone looks like our man Michael. Older gentleman but got the same looks."

"Not like me," Michael says.

"What's your last name?"

Michael starts painting. He acts like he doesn't hear him.

"White," I say.

Michael glares at me.

"Whitey," Jerome says. "They called the guy Whitey. Little rough around the edges."

"I don't have nothin' to do with that man," Michael says, and he sets his brush on a paint can and turns to Jerome, body tight as a bowstring.

The fight looks inevitable now. An alien overseer, passing by, gives us a hard stare. I turn to Jerome, but he isn't in fighting posture anymore. In fact, he looks kind of—I don't know—sad. He shakes his head. "Sorry, man. Really. I got me a daddy just like that. Wouldn't have brought it up if I'd known."

It's like something breaks in Michael then. He

backs up against the wall and slides down to the floor, where he sits with his legs sprawled out. He turns away from us. Jerome and I sit down, too. It's like we're all suddenly exhausted.

"My mom was a diabetic," Michael says.

We all know what this means. Anyone with any kind of physical illness was killed in the first attack.

"She was a wonderful woman and she's dead, and that cockroach survives. All the good people are dead."

I don't agree, but this isn't a time to argue. We sit quietly, even Jerome. After a while we start painting again. When a bad thing happens, a terrible thing, you feel it all the time, but you don't have a choice after a while. You go on anyway. I never would have understood that before. It's something I would have been happy to live my whole life without understanding.

««««(7)»»»»

The aliens have set up tables and a cafeteria line in what used to be a fancy dining room. It has big doors out onto a patio, big stained wood cabinets, and a gigantic chandelier that hangs at the center of the room.

I see the girl who kissed me that morning sitting at a table. I tell Michael to follow me.

"That the kissing girl?" Michael says as we pass between the tables.

I nod. "On the cheek."

"Not bad, Tex."

"It wasn't that way."

"What way was it?"

I don't have an answer. We sit across from her. I'm a little shy for some reason. Michael grins. He's enjoying my embarrassment, the *illegitimate son*. He introduces himself and me. Her name is Lauren DeVille.

Lauren seems shy, too, but she gets over it quickly, which puts me at ease. She tells us about her job in the kitchen. She preps food and works lunch. She tells us about an alien named Addyen who she works for. She says Addyen actually talks to her like she isn't an animal, like she isn't a stupid cow or something. She's one alien who isn't so bad, according to Lauren.

"They're all bad," Michael says.

"But the food is good," I say. True. The aliens can cook.

"Who's that?" Michael says. He's looking at the girl I noticed the other day, the one who looks a little like Paris Hilton: same long legs, thin body, and long blond hair.

"Lindsey," Lauren says. "She's supposed to be some model or something. Was a model. Total narcissist."

"What?" Michael says, watching the girl walk to a seat. She does know how to walk.

"Someone in love with themselves," I say.

"I knew that," he says with his mouth full. He looks down at his empty plate. "The food is pretty good, but there's not enough of it."

"They believe they give us an amount sufficient for our dietary needs," Lauren says, which is the way they talk. "At least everyone gets something," she adds.

"At least now a fourth of the world's population isn't starving or underfed. In a weird way, it's more fair."

"Most people are dead," Michael points out.

To me that kind of says it all. Not to Lauren.

"Of course that's terrible," she says, like he's stating the obvious but missing her point. "I'm just saying no one has so much food they let half of it go to waste while other people are starving. This house is an example of how one person took up the resources of thousands. It's obscene."

"It's an awesome house," Michael says.

She frowns and tells us she read an article about the original owner of this house. He was into strip mining and oil drilling and even the stolen diamond trade in Africa. He would do anything to make his millions.

Listening to her depresses me even more. This guy was like the poster child for the ways humans are unworthy of survival.

"Well," Michael says, standing, "it's been enlightening."

As in *not*, of course.

"I'm sorry," she says to me as Michael leaves. "It was his calling this place awesome that set me off. I can get sort of militant about certain issues."

"I understand," I say.

We take our trays up to the line. Lauren gets

Michael's, which he left. When we part, there's a slight hesitation.

"I'll see you around," I say. She smiles. The smile reminds me a little of that sad smile from the morning, a fainter version. Then she's gone.

(((((8)))))

I have a hard time sleeping that night. I keep hearing crying. A soft, smothered sound that I decide is coming from a girl. The strange thing is that the sound isn't coming from outside me. I hear it in my head. I get a little freaked. I mean, sure, I can hear the Handlers when they send me a message. But the crying isn't coming from a Handler, and I can still hear it. I think back to earlier, when I saw that image of Jerome fighting in a bar. What is happening to me?

I know something else somehow. The girl is alone in a room, which is odd because no humans sleep alone in this place.

I hear Michael stir. Then he starts snoring softly. After a while the girl stops crying, or I stop being able to hear her.

It's crazy that I could hear a girl crying in my mind, but I'm in Crazy World now. It's hard to know what anything means.

I wish for about the thousandth time that I could talk to my dad. It's not like I don't want to see my mom, too, but it's my dad's advice I need. I'd ask him, "When the world has gone crazy, how do you keep yourself from following it?"

Since all I hear is silence, I have to imagine what he'd say.

"The world has always been crazy, Grasshopper."

My dad was a big fan of any TV show or movie that had martial arts in it. That included this ridiculous show from the seventies called *Kung Fu*. Kwai Chang Caine is the main character, who grew up in a monastery in China, and his master, when he gave advice, always called him Grasshopper. My dad adopted the name for me when he gave me advice. Sometimes it was funny. Most of the time it was irritating.

"Yeah," I say to Dad, "but invasion-by-little-green-telepathic-aliens crazy?"

"You've got a point."

"How can I hear a girl crying in my head?"

"You could be crazy," he admits.

He could be right.

"I wish you were here," I say, and that wish feels like something cold inside me, something so cold it hurts.

"Me too."

"You'd know what to do."

"No," he says. "I'd be just like you. I'd be trying to figure it out. The goal is to stay alive and keep trying to figure it out."

He's right. I say, "I think I hear the girl because she's here in this house somewhere. Maybe it's crazy, but that's what I think."

"Smart boy," he says.

And he's gone. And I'm alone.

(((((9)))))

LORD VERTENOMOUS

To Senator & High Lord Vertenomous:

Congratulations on having the colony named in your honor. I am confident Vertenomousland will be a great success. The nonhearing species will make excellent labor slaves because of their size. They could be exported to farming or industrial colonies. The hearing will, of course, bring higher prices, and since we didn't expect this level of hearing, our profits will be higher than originally thought. I did not mean to sound concerned about the hearing product. They are primitive. They only hear when we send them direct, amplified messages through links. I believe we can expect great things from this colony over time.

I will keep you informed, Senator.

ATTACHED NOTE TO THE OFFICIAL CORRESPONDENCE:

Father,

You misunderstand me, sir. I am not asking for special treatment concerning my family. Nor am I complaining about conditions on this colony. Perhaps I only asked because of our conversation not long before I struck out on my mission. We sat in your study and drank Sumbulla, and you reminisced about your first assignment. You spoke of your passion for your first wife, how you felt the lack of her like a wound. I was deeply moved. Perhaps this was on my mind when I expressed my desire to have my wife and daughters here.

As for the product: of course I am aware that it is best if religious and product-rights groups do not learn of these hearing humans until the colony is settled. I will be, as you advise, careful in my reports.

I have taken one of the product as a second. She is superior to the others in both beauty and ability to hear. She is small and desirable. Hardly any taller than our own females, in fact. As you have mentioned in the past, it is good to have a second to keep one's focus when away from one's spouse. Also, it does give insight into the species.

I have studied her, particularly when she dreams. It is very curious. I do not know of another primitive culture that dreams. It is not true power, of course, but it is an altered state, a separate existence within the mind. Their experiences, apparently, seem real to them while they dream. This does not make them less primitive, because it is an illusion and contained within each unit, but it is interesting.

I look forward to your first visit. I will have much to show you.

10

Michael, Lauren, and I are sitting on one of the sofas in the library after dinner, the one time of day we get a little break. Lauren is telling us that Benjamin Franklin owned slaves, which is disappointing. The girl does know a lot about a lot.

Lindsey passes by with her sidekicks. At the same time, a girl who's overweight gets up from a chair. Lindsey says, loud enough everyone can hear, "Porker."

Lindsey's sidekicks giggle. It's like some bad teen movie.

The overweight girl turns bright red and lowers her eyes.

"Some things haven't changed," Lauren says.

"She was a model, right?" Michael says.

"She says she's been in a lot of magazines, but I've

never seen her. I don't read those kinds of magazines much though."

"She's pretty hot," Michael says. "I could see her as a model."

"Typical guy. You've just seen her showing what a vain, self-centered creep she is and what do you say? *She's pretty hot.*"

"Everyone has faults."

He's staring at Lindsey, who has settled at a table by some bookcases; she notices. He smiles. She smiles.

"God," Lauren says.

Lindsey tosses her hair back. She's one of those girls who gets a lot out of a hair toss.

"You know what's got her so upset," Lauren says. "The aliens don't think she's totally hot. They think she's big."

"She's not big," I say.

"She's tall. They like their girls tiny. They assigned her to laundry. She wanted to be their personal secretary or something, but they told her no. And they call her big. That really gets her."

"So she's a porker to them," I say.

"Maybe that's why she said that to the girl," Michael says. "See, I'm not really so shallow. I get the psychology of the whole thing. I think I'm gonna have to go over there and talk to her, help her understand what's bothering her."

"God," Lauren says again.

He's smiling and he puts up a fist. What can I do? I won't leave a friend hanging. We touch fists, and off he goes.

"You boys," Lauren says, more playful than I'd expect.

"Don't put me with him. I'm not part of the Lindsey fan club."

"I know." She looks kind of thoughtful then. "What do you think you would have been part of?"

"What do you mean?"

"If all this hadn't happened, what would you have, you know, become?"

"I don't know."

"What would you have studied in college?"

"Probably English. I don't know for sure, though."

Lauren does, of course. She knows everything. Double major: English and biology. Then she would have gone into the Peace Corps. She'd come back and go to medical school. She'd work for Doctors Without Borders or some other international group that helps those who can't afford medical treatment.

"You would have been a great doctor," I say.

"Thank you," she says.

"For what?"

"I don't know. Letting me talk about it. Pretending I have a future."

A Handler passes by.

"You have a future."

"Right," she says. "Someone's slave. That's my future."

"Maybe not," I say, but I believe she's right. I don't want to but I do.

"You know better, Jesse. We're going to be their slaves until we die. Just look around. They're everywhere. There's no way we can get away from this."

"They aren't everywhere," I say. "They seem like they are, but they aren't."

"I'm afraid they are," she says with the confidence of a straight-A student. "I feel them. If you try, you can feel them."

"That's the way it seems," I say.

She looks slightly confused. "What do you mean?"

"Some nights I study their movements. My dad was big on observation. He was always telling me to really look at things. When I look closely, some of them fade, like they're not real, like they're phantoms. The aliens make them to make us feel like they're everywhere."

I lean closer to her. "Look at the one by the chair. Keep looking. Really look at it."

Lauren stares at it, and after a few seconds, I can see that she sees it disappear.

"Unbelievable," she says. She sits back. She taps the sofa with her fingers and for a second I'm reminded of Mr. Whitehead and the day of the invasion. "So maybe you're right. Maybe they're not omnipotent, but they took over our world in ten seconds. I'm not sure it matters if they're everywhere or just *almost* everywhere."

"It matters," I say. "There's a difference between omnipotent and *almost* omnipotent."

We're ordered to bed. She smiles and for just a second I think she might kiss me again. I can almost see a future of kisses from her, and it's almost like I have something to look forward to. It doesn't happen. She stands up. She says, "You're right." I should have kissed her is what I think. Then I think, *What am thinking?* This isn't the time for kissing or finding a girlfriend. This is the time to focus on staying alive.

"There is a difference," she says at the top of the stairs. "Thank you, Jesse." Survival is important, but even so, I'm still thinking about that almost-kiss as I head off to my room.

11

I'm dreaming. I know I'm dreaming.

I hear the girl crying again. Her crying is hushed, like she's crying into a pillow or something. She stops abruptly. "Is someone there?" I don't think she can be talking to me because I'm not there. I'm here in a bedroom that has the sweaty sock smell of a locker room.

"Who's there?" she says.

"Are you talking to me?" I say. I can't see her.

"Who else would I be talking to?"

"Right," I say. "My dream, after all. You should be talking to me."

"Are you trying to be funny?" she says. Something about her voice makes me think she's cute. Maybe it's a strange thing to think under the circumstances, but I'm pretty sure most guys would notice. I guess if I were in front of a firing squad and the squad was made up of all girls, my last thought might be, "That one on the end is kind of cute."

"Not really," I say.

"Who are you?"

"Look, it's my dream. Shouldn't I be asking the questions?"

"It's not really a should or shouldn't situation. Anyway, it could be my dream."

"I guess."

"But I think it's yours. It doesn't feel like one of mine." She says this matter-of-factly as if she's been in someone else's dream before.

"Where are you?" I say.

"In a tower that's not a tower."

"A tower that's not a tower," I repeat. "That sounds like dream talk."

"Maybe you've come in a dream because that's the only way to get to me. You don't know how to come any other way, right?"

"I don't know."

"You don't know what?"

"What you're talking about."

"Maybe we should try something. Imagine you're next to me. Just imagine that."

"Okay." This is strange, but dreams are strange, right? I do what she asks. I imagine myself next to her.

Immediately, I'm in another room, standing next to a small, pretty girl. The moonlight slips through big bay windows, and I can see that she has straw-colored hair and enormous green eyes.

"I'm Catlin," the girl says. "I don't know how you broke through, but I'm glad to see you."

"You're in the house, Lord Vertenomous's, aren't you?"

"Yes."

"My dad was right."

"Your dad's here?" she says, looking around.

"No. Not—never mind. How are we having this conversation?"

"We're in your dream. It's not ideal," she says, "but I'm still glad to see you."

She's tiny but something about her seems large somehow. She puts her hand on my arm and tugs slightly, and I sit next to her on the bed.

"I need you to remember me when you wake," she says.

"Who are you, though?"

"I need someone to know I'm alive because sometimes, locked up here, it feels like I'm not. I need to be sure someone remembers."

"I'll remember," I say, though it does cross my mind that I might not. I don't always remember my dreams.

Then I have a feeling. I've been having a lot of these feelings lately. The feeling is this: Lord Vert has been here recently.

"This is his room, isn't it?" I say. I jump off the bed. I'm worried that I've walked into a trap, that the girl has lured me here.

"Not exactly, but you'd better go," she says. "He could be coming."

"Why would he come here if it's not his room?"

"Go," she says.

Then, somehow, she sends me away. I'm falling.

"Remember me," she shouts.

I wake up.

At first I don't remember what I was dreaming. Someone farts. It is probably the longest fart I've ever heard. Not that I'm an expert on farts, though sharing a room with this many guys is definitely giving me more experience in that area than I ever wanted. The guy's extreme fart does not improve the odor of our room.

Then I suddenly remember the girl. I remember talking to her and I remember sitting on her bed and I even remember the feeling that Lord Vert had been there. She's real, and she's somewhere in this house.

««««(12)»»»»

LORD VERTENOMOUS

To Senator & High Lord Vertenomous:

No, my implication was not that there might be a situation remotely similar to what happened in Sector 301. That primary species was advanced. This one is primitive.

I've picked the most advanced of their species I can find to be placed in my own house for observation. They have shown no unanticipated mental abilities.

My memory of the species in Sector 301 is that their contact with us caused latent talents to develop in them. Nothing like that has happened. I am finding that this species may be capable of a kind of primitive shield. Not something they can control. Something that is built into them. This causes the shadows I spoke of earlier. It may cause us some minor problems, but I do not anticipate that it will interfere with any of the delivery deadlines.

To Senator & High Lord Vertenomous:

Other houses have been alerted to be especially vigilant in observation of the species. We are proceeding as scheduled. I will say this: The species has very strong and often raw emotions. Everything is so direct in them. It is both attractive and repellent. Have you encountered this in other species?

To Senator & High Lord Vertenomous:

Of course I am not going native. Yes, I do enjoy my second, but she is only a slave. I spoke of their raw emotions only as an odd feature of their primitive minds. It is good to study product so that we may improve our teaching techniques.

To Senator & High Lord Vertenomous:

There has been an incident, a casualty actually. A patrol in Section 3, a remote, semidesert area just west of my position, did not make his report this morning. Another patrol was sent to the last-known coordinates, and they found his body. He'd been killed by one of their crude weapons. We are investigating, but there have been other problems in Section 3 that indicate some of the product is still loose there. It is annoying, but I see no real threat. I will increase patrols, and we will find and exterminate them.

To Senator & High Lord Vertenomous:

The product that killed the patrol has been captured. Two males. They claim to have come upon the patrol and to have killed him before he felt their presence. They claim to have had no contact with others. Unfortunately, when they were being brought back for interrogation, they managed to kill themselves by jumping from the transport device. We are investigating how it was possible for them to make such a move without the patrol in the transport knowing before they acted.

To Senator & High Lord Vertenomous:

I have communicated with the other house heads. We will be ready by the earlier shipping date you have ordered. No section head has indicated a problem, though there is, as to be expected, some minor resistance to new deadlines. All will be ready.

We're in the library, sitting on a sofa. Most of the others have gone to their bedrooms without beds.

"Look," Michael says, "there's no comparison between the two sports. You look like you're making out when you're wrestling. Like you're kissing and hugging another guy. It's not a real sport."

"It's in the Olympics. Is football in the Olympics?" I say.

"Football is an American sport."

"Yeah, well, there is no America anymore." I'm sorry I say this the second it comes out. I want to take it back. "Anyway. Olympics. Real sport."

"I could see boxing. I mean, it's not as exciting as football, but it's a sport. You ever boxed?"

"A wrestler will always beat a boxer. If their skill levels are the same, I mean. The wrestler just has to get inside the boxer's range and take him off his feet and he's helpless as a little baby. But they're the same in one way. You do them alone. It's all up to you. No team stuff. You don't have to rely on anyone. I like that."

"My man Tex is not a team player."

"I don't like team think. It's fine on the football field, but it never stops there. It gets into everything."

"Does anyone even watch wrestling? I suppose they watch *Friday Night SmackDown* or something. That kind of wrestling maybe."

"Real wrestling is an old sport. The Greeks did it."

"The Greeks?" he says, disgusted.

"You take people down in football. You tackle them, right?"

"I make people miss. Maybe you've seen the game? Running back. He gets the ball and runs down the field and people try to tackle him. Of course, other people block for him. Those would be his teammates."

"I played football as a sophomore."

"But quit because Tex can't play with others."

"I can. I just don't like to."

"People watch football," he says. "More people watch the Superbowl than vote."

"I don't know if that's actually true," I say. It sounds like it might be, though.

"They love you for it if you're good. I was good, Tex. That was the one thing I could do better than anyone."

"Yeah," I say. "I know you were good."

"Sometimes I don't think I can stand this."

I'm silent then. He's spoken the unspeakable, and I'm afraid to say anything.

I think of my father saying *What's important, Grasshopper, is how you blend the skills you have when you're in a real fight. Everything else is just play, sport, or entertainment.* That was my dad. He'd been in that place where he'd had to fight for his life, and he'd survived because of what he did and what he knew. To me martial arts and wrestling were about a lot of things: skill, pride, focus, accomplishment, but I didn't really understand what my father meant. Now I do.

"Maybe you can wrestle your way out of here, Tex," Michael says.

"Maybe you can run your way out."

A Handler comes over and tells us to go to our room.

"It's not time," I say.

Reason number fifty why I would never join the military is that I have a problem with authority. (I gave my dad fifty reasons when he tried to convince me to join up). I suppose it is this character flaw that causes me to mess with the Sans in dangerous ways, even though I'm not gaining anything by it.

"Go to your room," the Handler says, and he has that look they get when they won't put up with much, a look that feels like a gun pointed at your head.

"Come on," Michael says. He grabs my arm and pulls me toward the stairs.

Upstairs in our room, I ask Michael if he thinks they were listening to us. There's a rumor going around that an alien was killed by rebels out west somewhere, and I think they've been watching us more closely. Michael says there are no rebels, that it's just wishful thinking.

He says, "Anyway, why would they care what we say?"

"Maybe they're worried. Maybe there *are* rebels."

"There are no rebels," he says again.

But here's the thing I think later. If they're worried, there must be a reason they're worried. I know that when you're in a wrestling match and you think you're beat, you'll lose. It's true in martial arts and football for that matter, too. People convince themselves into losing all the time. The best, in terms of strength and talent, don't always win. It may even be the biggest reason sports are interesting.

We think the Sans can't be defeated, but what if

we've convinced ourselves we have no chance and so we have no chance? What if there are rebels out west that haven't been killed or captured by the self-proclaimed most powerful beings in the known universe? It would change things. Just the thought is like a warm blanket on a cold night to me. Maybe we aren't helpless.

«««((14)))»»»

The next night, as I head up to our room, I see Michael coming out of the couples' room (that's what they call the room where they allow us to hook up) with Lindsey. They're both smiling and they kiss and say their reluctant good-byes at the top of the stairs. I wait for Michael at the door to our bedroom.

"Dude," I say. "You didn't."

"I did," he says. "I did and did and did and—"

"Okay, I get it."

"That's one crazy girl," he says. "She told me she was making some kind of fuss the other day and one of the Handlers asked her if she wanted to be dead. You know what she said?"

"'No' would have been a good answer."

"She said, 'What do you frickin' think?'"

I shake my head, but I do have to admire her.

"She likes the way we look together. My black against her white and blond."

"That's so sweet," I say.

"Sometimes you sound like a girl," he says.

"Sometimes you sound like a dick."

"Better a dick than a girl."

"Shut up," I say.

He laughs. "Yeah, you're jealous. Tex is jealous."

"A little."

"She'd be perfect if she didn't talk so much," he says.

"That's just wrong," I say.

"Yeah, but it feels so right."

"Shut up," I say again.

He just laughs. He's in too good a mood for anything to disturb it. Then I really am jealous.

Lauren and I are eating dinner the next night. She's picking at her food. I ask her if she's all right.

"I was just missing my mom."

"I'm sorry," I say.

She smiles that sad smile of hers. "You would have liked her. She had a good sense of humor. She was an awesome nurse. She was always trying to get me to slow down, but she supported me in everything I did."

"She sounds great," I say.

"I miss her."

We're both silent then.

I see Michael come off the cafeteria line with his tray.

"Michael," I call.

He nods but doesn't come right away. I realize he's waiting for someone. Then I realize that that someone is Lindsey. They're smiling mindlessly at each other as they walk toward us.

"You've got to be kidding me," Lauren says.

Michael and Lindsey sit down. Lauren pretends to find her food, which is some kind of vegetarian stew, fascinating. "This is really good," Michael says. "Even my mother would have to admit this is really good."

Michael eats, well, like a football player. He shovels food in. His spoon bangs against his bowl like the ringing of a bell. Within a brief minute or two, everything is gone. He looks like he might eat the bowl, too, but he controls himself.

Lindsey, meanwhile, has taken only a few hesitant bites. Small ones. She chews with obvious relish, though she keeps looking at the stew suspiciously. She pushes it away. Then she pulls it back and takes another little bite.

"If you don't want it," Michael says, "I'll be happy to finish it for you."

"It's hard for anyone to eat with you acting like a vulture ready to grab their food," Lauren says to Michael.

I'm surprised Lauren's defending Lindsey. Michael looks hurt, but Lindsey looks relieved. It's not like she digs in, though. She continues her tiny bites and her ritual of pushing the bowl away and pulling it back.

Michael studiously looks away. He's pretty obviously still interested in her food. If she pushes that bowl too far once, I'm not sure she'll get it back.

Lauren tells us that she helped make the stew. She tells us Addyen talks to her about stuff, like her religion and how she wants to open her own restaurant one day. Like before, Lauren talks like the alien is a friend, which is irritating.

"She's not your friend," I say.

"I never said she was. She's just not like the others, that's all."

Lindsey pushes her bowl away. "She's an alien. She's one of them. They ruined everything. I was about to get in a Victoria's Secret catalog. You know who I was going to have dinner with this month? Donald Trump."

Lauren's eyes narrow. Their truce is obviously over. "This whole invasion has been one big inconvenience for you, hasn't it?"

"As a matter of fact, it has been," Lindsey snaps. "It's the biggest inconvenience in the history of the frickin' world."

"That's probably true," I say.

Michael snorts and Lindsey gives a small laugh. Even Lauren smiles.

As we bus our trays, Lauren says, "Addyen asked me to stop by the kitchen after dinner. Why don't you come with me? I want you to see what she's like." I see she really wants me to meet Addyen, so I agree. We sneak back to the kitchen. Addyen is sitting at a table. She's not taller than most of the female aliens, but she is wider.

"Lauren," she says, surprised.

"You told me to come by," Lauren reminds her.

She looks at me. "Not him. If one of the Handlers finds him here, there will be trouble. Anchise is watching this part of the house."

Anchise is the worst of the Handlers. He likes hurting people.

"Maybe we should leave," I say.

Addyen stands. "Stay," she says. It's not like she says the word in an unkind way or anything. It's just that it sounds a lot like the way I used to say "stay" to my dog.

In a few seconds she's back with bowls and a container. She scoops something into the bowls and passes them to us with spoons. We eat. It's cold like ice cream, but it's not ice cream. It's impossible to describe because it's like nothing I've ever eaten, but it actually makes me feel good.

"We're not all like Lord Vertenomous or the Handlers," Addyen says as we eat. "You may have good masters when the settlers arrive. You may have lives that are not so hard."

Good masters. That's the best we can hope for now. I'm about to say something when another cook comes in. She looks horrified to see us. Not looks. She doesn't look any different, but I feel what she feels.

"Perhaps you better go," Addyen says.

"Thanks for the dessert," I say.

I admit on the way back to the library that Addyen isn't so bad for an alien. We find Michael and Lindsey and talk for a while, almost like friends at school. I feel almost, I don't know, normal.

Lindsey and Lauren even agree that women shouldn't wear fur. Lauren is a dog person and Lindsey is a cat person, but they both think the idea of wearing animal fur is wrong and gross.

"It's like that commercial where the actress says you wouldn't wear your dog."

"Or your cat," Lindsey says. "A lot of famous people are totally for animal rights."

"I volunteered in a shelter. You wouldn't believe some of the things I've seen."

No big surprise that Lauren volunteered in a shelter. I wonder if there is anyplace she didn't volunteer.

Lindsey says, "You know who else is all over animal rights? Paris and Alicia. I know them."

"You know them?" Michael says.

"Well, I've met them, anyway."

The conversation becomes a little bit of a tug-of-war. Lauren talks about animal cruelty, like using bunnies to test cosmetics or monkeys to test drugs. Things like that. Lindsey talks more about any famous person who cares about animals. After a few minutes of this, we're ordered to bed by a Handler. Lindsey and Lauren go on talking as we move up the stairs.

When we get to our room, Michael says, "Are they actually becoming friends?"

"I wouldn't go that far," I say, "but it's weird. I thought they hated each other."

"You can't tell with girls, dude. I'm not saying they're as different as the aliens, but they're more than halfway there."

We nod silently at the wisdom of these words.

(((((16)))))

I see Catlin again that night. I'm dreaming, and I know I'm dreaming. She's standing at the window in the moonlight wearing a short nightgown. I can see her body more clearly. She has nice legs.

"How is this happening?" I say. I'm standing by the door. The room seems enormous from this angle.

"You're making it happen," she says.

"How?"

She shrugs. She has a small round face, which her short, straight hair crowds; she pushes her hair back when it slips over her eyes.

"I don't know. Lord Vertenomous put a locking spell on this room. He wouldn't call it a spell, but I do. I can't break it. You can, somehow."

"In my dream," I say.

Catlin nods. "He feels someone has been here, but he can't believe it. He can't believe even a Handler could break his spell."

"You're saying they use magic?"

"They wouldn't call it that. They use their minds. But it's like magic, isn't it? Magic from inside."

"Why are you here?" I ask. *I wonder if she's human.*

"Of course I'm human," she says sharply.

My face heats and I feel a little blush. I hate that. *You read my mind? If you are human how can you read it like they do?*

"You know how," she says. "I hope you aren't one of those people who pretends not to know what you know."

"I know you're not like me," I say stubbornly. "We can't read minds without alien help."

"I think maybe I am like you, Jesse," she says.

"How do you know my name?"

"That doesn't matter. Here's something that does. You're right about the rebels. There are rebels."

"How could you know that?" I'm suspicious of her. I think of Lauren, and I know she would tell me to be careful. She would point out the nature of simple math and say there are things about this girl that don't add up.

"I don't know who Lauren is, but you came to me; I didn't come to you."

I realize I have to be careful what I think around this girl. "But how do you know there are rebels?" I say.

"I know a lot of things," she says. "Get me out of here and I'll tell you more."

"For example?"

She looks at me like I'm trying to take advantage of her, but then she shrugs and seems to relax a little.

"Those rebels out west killed that patrol. I think they were able to sneak up on him."

"How? The aliens can hear us."

"Maybe there are ways to keep them from hearing. Maybe the rebels know some of those ways."

"How?"

"Get me out."

"How can I get you out? I don't even know where we are. In a dream. That's all I know."

"You can get in," she says. "You can get yourself out. Figure out a way to take me with you. We can't stay here."

"What do you mean?"

"We're going to have to make a run for it sooner or later. You're going to have to. You know I'm right."

I know we'd be turned off in a second. How could we even get out of the house without them knowing? I realize that when I think this, even though I'm mostly thinking how impossible it is, I think *we*, not *I*. I'd want to take my friends. That is, if I ever tried anything so crazy.

I'm about to tell the girl this when I hear something. Actually it's not as much a sound as it is the absence of sound, like a hole in sound. A shadow moves toward us. Cold. Really cold. It's as if I'm suddenly outside on a winter night without a coat. I shiver. Catlin shivers, too.

"Go," Catlin whispers through chattering teeth.

I try to will myself back to my room, but I can't. The shadow gets closer and darkens. I take a step back, but that's no good. It's moving fast. It starts to slip over me. Only then do I manage to get back to my room. It's kind of like I'm in a *Star Trek* movie and I'm beamed back.

The shadow follows, covering the room. Everyone wakes up because it's so cold. Everyone is suddenly in a winter night. It lingers. Only as it leaves do I see it transform.

"What the hell was that?" Michael says.

"Did you see it?"

"See what? I felt it get really, really cold. I didn't see anything."

But I did. I saw the shadow become Lord Vert. I could hear him then. It wasn't a thought exactly. It was more like a feeling, his feeling that it was impossible one of us could have been in that room with his spell on it. Impossible.

"What did you see?" Michael says.

I don't tell him about Lord Vert. Instead, I tell him I saw a girl in a dream.

"Was she pretty?"

"Oh, yeah."

"You start groaning in your sleep, I'm waking you up," he says.

"I just met her."

He frowns at me. He shakes his head. "She's a girl in a dream. What does it matter?"

We're all shivering as we lie back down. Then I have a thought that warms me a little. Lord Vert, leader of the all-powerful Sanginians, is wrong. One of us—me—was in his room. One of us—me—did the impossible, which makes it possible, which makes me wonder what else might be possible. Maybe it isn't so crazy to think of escape, after all.

I have a rule that I've tried to follow since I started high school. Don't be a follower or a leader. I have lots of friends and I'm loyal, but I go my own way. Michael's saying I wasn't a team player was at least partly right. But I believe something now the others don't believe. I believe the aliens aren't invincible. I've got to convince my friends that I'm right. Of course I'm aware of one little problem. If I'm wrong, we all die.

(((((17)))))

LORD VERTENOMOUS

Personal Log:

A patrol ship and officer in Section 3a are missing. I have sent two patrol ships to investigate. It is possible we missed, in our scouting reports, some type of natural phenomenon that might be dangerous to us.

I see no reason to report this to the company. The settlement is proceeding as planned. Soon the first wave of colonists will arrive. Everything will be fine. No, I won't report any trouble. Father would no doubt find time to criticize my concern. He has little time for me, but he makes time for criticism.

Last night I had a conversation with my

second, who calls herself Catlin. She wanted to know about the One. I knew she wouldn't understand, but I spoke to her, anyway, humored her, because of my affection for her. I described the One and how He is connected to all things as we are connected to all things. He speaks and hears as we speak and there are moments when the whole universe listens as one. He is supreme, and we are made in His image.

She said the One sounded like God, angering me. I scolded her. Then I tried to patiently explain. *The One is connected to all things and is all things and we are as He is because we are part of the One. You are not. You do not hear and you cannot speak. Your God is like the god of most primitives, a reflection of what you are. He is false.*

I was so patient in my explanation. But then she said our god was just like us, which meant He could be a reflection of us. I became very angry. Here was product, the unconnected, speaking blasphemy to me. It was too much. I nearly broke her mind, but I stopped myself at the last second. Still, I damaged her. I do not yet know how badly. I will learn today if she can be repaired. I hope so. She amuses me most of the time.

(((((18)))))

We're working outside, painting.

"It's not the same," I say.

"It's the same," Michael says.

"No," I say, "it isn't."

"Why isn't it the same?"

"They set the whole thing up," I say. "How is that real?"

"They had to set up the situation. But then what happened, happened. Like life, Tex."

"I don't think so. I think they scripted parts of it."

"What do you mean, scripted?" Michael says.

"They learned lines for situations. Not the whole thing but some situations."

"No way. *Survivor?* Those people were serious."

"Even if they didn't script it, or all of it," I say, "people were watching. That changed everything."

"They were real people, and they acted out. *Big Brother?* You put people like that in a house, and it will get crazy. Even if no one was watching, it would get crazy."

"I'm just saying they acted a certain way for the camera. It made a difference."

"That's still real," Michael says.

"They voted on who had to leave the house or island or whatever."

"Well, yeah, it was a competition. You got to have that."

"Like a game," I say.

"Right," Michael says. "It was a game."

"So it wasn't real."

"Reality TV," he says in a loud and totally obnoxious tone. "Not reality. It was real enough for TV."

He knows that he's on weak ground. He asks me what I watched, then, if I hated reality TV so much.

"I liked lots of things," I say.

"A guy like you who wouldn't watch reality television must have watched public TV and news shows and stuff like that, right?"

"Sometimes. I watched movies a lot. I'm a movie person. I was."

"So you've never seen that superhero show?"

"I watched that," I admit.

"Right. I knew it. Comic books, graphic novels, fantasy, and sci-fi. That's you."

"So? What's your point?"

"Shit, man, you're giving me a hard time about reality TV. Look at yourself. Look at what you watched. You talk about something not being real."

"Oh, I don't know," I say. "Doesn't seem so far off now."

Michael looks over at a Handler. "They were still lame shows."

Then he adds, *Lame like you.*

You're just bitter about your lame defense of reality shows.

Only then do I realize that he didn't actually say "Lame like you" out loud. And I've answered without out speaking, just by thinking. We both stare at each other.

We're like them.

"No, we aren't," he says. Then he shouts it. "We aren't like them!"

He walks away.

(((((**19**)))))

I make friends with this white-haired woman named Betty who is the oldest person here. She used to be a college history teacher in Michigan. She tells me she's been keeping track of the days since the aliens came. The Sans have destroyed all calendars and clocks and watches because our way of breaking up time irritates them. Also, of course, they consider watches and clocks machines.

Betty may be the only one who knows what day it is.

I sit with her at lunch. I say, "What day is it, Betty?" I care because it's something from our world. More and more of our world disappears every day.

She looks like she may not remember me, but then she smiles. "It's my husband's birthday," she says.

"Your husband was sent somewhere else?" I say.

"Bad heart," she says. "We were together when they invaded. He fell asleep with the others. The big sleep as that noir writer called it."

I don't know what she's talking about but the memory of her husband dying twists up her face and I think she's about to cry.

"What day is it, Betty?" I say again.

She smiles a broken smile. "And tomorrow is the first day of spring."

Michael sits next to me just as Betty says this. "What did you say?"

"Tomorrow is officially spring in Texas," she says again. "It feels the way summer in Michigan feels, but here it's only spring."

"Can't be."

"I'm quite sure," she says. "I've been very meticulous. We historians like to keep our dates straight."

"Spring," Michael says, looking down at his tray.

"I would like to give you a happy spring present, Jesse," Betty says. "You remind me of my son when he was your age. Look for me tomorrow."

She gets up.

"You haven't eaten," I say.

"I don't eat their food."

She's thin, and her movements are stiff and unnatural. I worry because the aliens won't keep anyone alive who can't be of use to them. "What do you eat, then?"

"Only what they don't give me."

"Can I eat it?" Michael says.

She pushes her tray toward him and walks away.

"Kind of a strange old lady," Michael says, "but I think I might start eating with her every day."

I see Lauren putting her tray up on the cart near the kitchen and then walking toward the library. I get up just as Lindsey sits down.

"Don't leave on my account," she says.

"I'm not. I just need to tell Lauren something. Michael can tell you."

"Nothing to tell," Michael says.

"What?" Lindsey says.

"There *is* something to tell."

"The aliens just left one of the lines open or something. Why can't you let it alone, Jesse?"

"Because it means something," I say, walking away.

For some reason I think of my dad telling me the story of how he once nearly died in a desert. He was dying of thirst, and he almost gave up. He wanted to. Something kept him going. One foot in front of the other.

"If I'd given up, I never would have met your mother, love of my life, or had you for a son or seen a

Texas spring or done a million other things. You don't know what you might miss if you don't make it to the next day. It could be something pretty wonderful. So sometimes, no matter how bad it is, you have to just put one foot in front of the other and hope you make it to a better place."

That's what I'm trying to do now. It's true, I don't know if it really means anything, but I want to believe it does. I want to believe that there's a way out of here, just like there was a way out of the desert for my dad.

I find Lauren reading and I sit down beside her on a big leather sofa. Something about her looks particularly pretty. I can't say what it is exactly, but I feel it.

"What?" she says. "Do I have something on my face?"

I realize I'm staring. I must look ridiculous. "No. Nothing."

She rubs her face anyway. "Did I get it?"

"You got it," I say. What else can I say at that point?

"Thank you."

Lindsey and Michael come in. I guess Lindsey didn't eat much of her lunch, or maybe she pushed her plate too close to Michael and he inhaled it. They sit down on the sofa across from Lauren and me.

"Did he tell you?" Lindsey says, and doesn't wait for an answer. "They read each other's minds."

"I was about to tell her," I say.

"What do you mean?" Lauren says.

"It was just a few sentences," Michael says.

"Whatever," Lindsey says. "They did it. Like the aliens."

Lauren looks at me. "Why didn't you tell me?"

"I was just about to."

"That's good, isn't it?" Lauren says. "I mean, you did something only they can do."

"I don't know," I say, "but I think it's good."

"It's bull," Michael says. "We're not like them."

"I think it's good," Lindsey says. "I've thought I've heard things sometimes. Whispers, kind of. I thought maybe I was, you know, just hearing stuff that wasn't there. But maybe it was there."

"We're getting stronger," I say.

"You don't know that," Michael says.

"They aren't as strong as they think they are, and we're stronger than they think we are. They aren't invincible."

"Okay," Lauren says. "Maybe not. So what are you saying?"

"I'm saying we have a chance to escape. We need to start thinking like prisoners who can escape. We don't have to just accept we're going to be slaves the rest of our lives. We have a choice."

"Right," Michael says. "We can be dead. What a choice."

"I'm afraid he's right," Lauren says. "They conquered the world in ten seconds. We're just four people."

"But we aren't the same as we were," I say.

Everyone is silent. I can feel them considering this. Is it possible? What does it mean?

The Handler on duty, Anchise, interrupts our conversation and orders us back to work.

"I think your biological clock is off, Anchise," I say. "We still have five or ten minutes."

Lauren foolishly agrees with me.

Anchise picks us both up and shoves us roughly toward the door. Not physically. He does it with his mind. I can hear him thinking how nice it would be to turn us off and be done with it.

Are you reading me? he thinks, stopping, holding me where I am. It's like he's pinching my arms with his fingers. Among all the big-eyed freaks, his eyes are the most frightening; something about them makes me think of a lake full of snakes. His mind closes. It's like I was looking through a window and now it's a wall. I feel him in me, and it's all I can do to hide what I saw under another thought. It's like I've thrown a blanket over it.

He frowns. I can tell he thinks he must have been wrong. I can tell he thinks it's impossible for a human to read him. He lets me go.

Wrong again. Another of the all-powerful Sanginians is wrong. We *are* stronger. There's a power in me that the aliens can't believe I have. It's come alive because of them, but it feels like something that was there all along. As I go back to work, I can hear my father say, "That's your advantage, Grasshopper."

(((((20)))))

The next morning is cool, the fog so thick it's difficult to see. Lauren and I get out to the pool early for morning assignments. No one else is out there yet. We do this most mornings.

"You ever wish you could go back and do it again?" Lauren says.

"Do what?"

"Everything."

"Maybe sometimes. I guess I wish I'd paid more attention."

"You do pay attention. Most boys don't pay attention at all, but you do."

I allow her to criticize my gender without defense because she's made me an exception. Still, I have to set the record straight. "Thank you, Ms. DeVille, but I missed a lot."

A female Handler comes out. Then three girls. A boy. They start to line up.

"What would you change?" I ask.

"I would take more time just to be, I think. I was always doing something. Save the whales. Working at the animal shelter or Habitat for Humanity. Class president, all that school stuff. Volleyball. Big Sister. I was doing something every minute of every day. I just never was, you know, me. I don't even know who me really was."

More people come out the door. By then there are enough that the Handler orders us to make a line.

"There would have been time," I say.

"What?"

"If they hadn't come. There would have been time."

We're forced into the line then, pulled by the Handler. What I wanted to say was there would have been time for us to grow up.

21

Insomnia. I toss. I turn. Everyone else is asleep.

I need to see Catlin, but I can only see her when I dream, and I can't dream if I can't sleep.

And I can't.

Catlin has information. I don't know how, but she does. I need her information. I need to know more.

I try counting sheepdogs. My dog, Merlin, was a sheepdog, and I count them jumping a fence. I'm over five hundred before I finally slip off.

"It's about time," she says, sitting up in bed. She yawns and stretches.

"I couldn't get to sleep," I say.

"Have you figured out how to get me out of here?"

"Not yet."

She nods as if this is the answer she expects. I go over to her bed.

"I need your help," I say.

"When I was a little girl, I used to have flying dreams. I loved those dreams. I don't suppose you can fly in your dreams."

"I haven't tried."

Catlin shakes her head. "I think you'd drop like a rock. No, I don't think you can fly me out of here."

"You said we have to escape. How do we get out of this house?"

She laughs. "You could just walk out the front door."

"Could we?"

"Of course not. There are probably traps all around. You'd be dead in about two seconds."

"How do we get past the traps?"

"See, that's why you need me. I'll give you a chance. But you're going to have to get me out of here."

"Maybe I should just dream my way into Lord Vert's and get the key."

"A key won't help. Anyway, I think you'd get caught. He'd hear you. Something about our dreaming confuses them. You fooled him once, but you won't fool him again. You have a great talent but he's strong. He's really strong."

"What do you mean by talent?"

"Wouldn't you call it a talent?" she says quickly, but I feel like she's hiding something.

"I guess."

"Lord Vertenomous is worried. The rebels killed a patrol. He feels like the slaves might not be as weak as he thought. He keeps convincing himself that he must be wrong, but he's worried. I can feel that much."

"We aren't as weak," I say. "We can sometimes hear each other. I heard my friend Michael. I think maybe others are hearing more, too. We're different."

"Different how?"

"The static is gone when they talk to us. I feel things people are thinking, or emotions sometimes."

"So you're changing," she says.

"I guess."

"It will get stronger," she says. "You can speed up the process by trying to improve your skills."

"I'm not sure," I say.

But this isn't true. I know how to improve skills. I've done it all my life in martial arts.

"You want to get out of here alive?"

"Of course."

"You've got to practice hearing. Your friend, too."

"Do you think we can get out of here?"

"I don't know, but I know we won't have a chance unless we're as strong as we can be."

"How do you know all this?"

"You'd better go now. It's time. He'll be here soon."

Catlin looks down when she says this, embarrassed.

"I'll come back for you," I say.

"I'd like to believe that."

"We're friends." I don't know if this is true, but saying it makes it more true to me.

"All right," she says, and she puts out her hand. "You get me out. I'll get you out. Friends."

We shake hands.

"You've got to go now."

I think of my bedroom, and I'm back in it. Everyone is still asleep, including me. I will myself to wake because I'm frightened of seeing myself sleep. It's like I'm dead. But as soon as I try to wake, I do. I'm back in my body, looking around, listening to Michael snore.

My breathing is short and sharp. My throat is dry.

I guess people have been dreaming for thousands and thousands of years. I imagine people have had every kind of dream possible in that time. But has anyone ever dreamed like me? Have they crossed over into the waking world and talked to someone?

No one answers these questions, of course. Sometimes you ask questions even when you know no one will answer. I imagine that's been going on for thousands of years, too.

I fall asleep after a little while. I have another dream, but this isn't one I travel in. It's a dream of the past, of my parents and me in Taos, New Mexico. We're walking around the plaza. We're laughing. Tourists are going in and out of shops, people talking, a couple taking bites of ice cream from each other's cones. Then it's different. Something is very wrong. I look around and no one is there, not even my parents; the whole plaza is deserted. The stores are all empty, too, and they look like they've been deserted for a long time. It feels like the town has been abandoned.

I hear something. I can't see them but I hear whispers, and the whispers feel like someone calling me. Then all at once the calling stops. Everything becomes silent and still, and something powerful and angry is in the square with me, something terrible.

It pulls at me from all directions. It's like it's pulling me apart. I wake up with my heart racing.

22

Betty gets herself killed today.

She hands me something at lunch. She puts her hands over mine for a second and she whispers, "Happy spring, Jesse."

"Come and sit with me," I say.

"I can't," she says.

"Well," I say, "thanks for the gift."

"My pleasure. You know how old I am?"

"You look young."

"Such a liar," she says, "but the good kind of liar. I'm sixty-one. I doubt there are many left who are sixty-one."

"You are."

"I am. I'm too old to see a future, Jesse."

I start to tell her what my dad told me, but she holds up her hand. "Keep track of the days. It's important. If there's a future, it will be important."

She walks away. I look at what she's given me: pages. At first I hardly recognize it: the little squares with numbers and days of the week. She's made a calendar. It begins with the date of the invasion. There are empty pages for the next year and a pencil to fill them in with. It's a funny thing, but seeing the calendar makes me hopeful. It's like seeing it makes me think there will be days in the future.

I look up as Betty approaches Anchise, and I know what she's going to do before she does it.

"No, Betty," I whisper.

She slaps Anchise so hard I can hear the surprise in Anchise's mind. I can hear her laughing even though I don't think she's laughing out loud. She looks back at me.

Anchise is going to kill her, turn her off like all the others, but something unbelievable happens. She stops him. It's not for long, just a second maybe, but long enough that I see it. She wants me to see it. This is part of my gift.

Then Anchise, the anger like fire in him, turns her off. He makes her scream in pain before she dies, but she doesn't stop looking him right in the eye. This makes him even more angry. I feel her leave. I can actually feel her move out of her body. Where does she go?

I feel sorrow defeat me. It's like it covers me. I get weak everywhere. I want to fall off my chair and curl up on the floor and just lie there. I can't stand this losing anymore. I can't.

But I do, and when I do, I get mad. "Why did you have to do that, Betty?" I want to shout at her corpse. I want to scream at it. "You are stupid! You are a coward! You make me sick! I hate you!" I want to say all these things to her.

Anchise doesn't say he's sorry. He turns and walks away, and I'm sure if anyone makes a noise, he will kill them, too. He can't control himself. She made him unable to control himself.

I put her calendar in my pocket, and my anger weakens and then disappears entirely.

"I'm sorry, Betty," I whisper.

She stopped Anchise. It was only for a second and she had to die to do it, but she stopped him. Betty wanted me to see that it could be done. She wanted me to see that they aren't invincible.

(((((23)))))

The next day, Michael and I are painting in the dorms again. Another day or two and we'll be done. The Handler supervising the crew wants us to think he's nearby, but I know better. I've improved at recognizing the phantoms they create, and I know that what's in the room with us isn't real.

"Betty stopped Anchise before he killed her," I say. "Did you feel it?"

"Maybe," Michael says. "I'm not sure."

"She did."

"Okay, let's say she did. One small point."

"What?"

"Betty's dead."

"We can run," I say. "We won't fight them directly. When we get stronger, then we'll fight."

"I can run, Tex. You just sort of walk fast."

I ignore this remark. "We steal a car."

"And go where?"

"West," I say. "We find the rebels and join them."

That's when I know where we have to go. I feel it.

"We go to Taos. There are a lot of places to hide in those mountains around Taos, and I know the area."

Michael says, "You might as well say the moon."

"Why would we want to go to the moon?"

"Shut up," he says.

Sometimes he's so easy to irritate it's almost not worth the effort. Almost.

"We get out of the cities. We get to a place where there aren't that many of them. You heard what Lauren said."

Lauren told us that when she was bused south from Chicago, she didn't see any aliens at all between cities. The country felt abandoned. But nothing was abandoned, of course. It was all taken from us.

"So that's your plan?" Michael says. "Steal a car and drive west? You must have thought long and hard to come up with so detailed a plan."

"Taos, New Mexico." I feel like that's where we need to go. I feel it strongly. It's almost like I can hear something in Taos, a whisper, calling me. I sure don't tell Michael about this because I know what he would say. "Shut up."

"It's a long drive to Taos, right?"

"It's a long, hard, hot drive," I admit. "But no worries. They'll probably kill us before we can get off the grounds anyway."

"I'm guessing you weren't on the debate team at your high school," he says.

A Handler comes in then, so I really do shut up.

When I meet Lauren in line for dinner that night, she puts her arms around me and hugs me.

"I'm sorry," she says.

I'm about to say that it isn't a big deal, that I didn't even really know Betty. But then I feel something very close to a tear on my cheek. Maybe it actually is a tear.

I push the feeling away and get out of her hug. "I have something to tell all of you."

By then Michael and Lindsey have joined us. I tell them all everything I know. I leave out the source of my information about the rebels, but I tell them they're out there and they killed a Sans.

"How do you know all this?" Lauren says.

"You just have to trust me."

I've chosen to make my escape pitch right as we sit down so that Michael's mouth will be full. There's so much food being stuffed in there that I know he won't be able to object.

"We're not helpless, and they're not invincible," I say. "We've got to try to escape."

"You really think it's possible?" Lauren says.

"My dad used to say that ordinary people can do extraordinary things in extraordinary times. That's where we are. I think it's possible."

"We'll need supplies," Lindsey says.

Lauren and I both look at her. She shrugs. "Anything is better than staying here."

Michael decides that he has to say something even if his mouth is mostly full. "They're too strong, too fast." He swallows. "It's like we're a high school football team going out to play the Super Bowl winners."

I'm pleased to see the girls aren't impressed by this sports analogy.

Lauren says, "I heard something today. Addyen told me that her husband will arrive soon. He's on a ship a couple days away."

"So?" I say.

"He's not coming alone. He's with a million aliens. A fleet of ships that's going to land in just a few days."

"Frick," Lindsey says.

Michael actually stops eating.

"It gets worse," she says. "There are millions more behind them. I asked Addyen, and she said maybe thirty million less than a year away."

"So many?" I say. It's like I've been punched in the gut. I have to take deep breaths.

"It doesn't matter," Lindsey says.

"It matters," I say. "There won't be any room for us."

"Like what happened to the Native Americans," Lauren says. "They were so outnumbered, they had nowhere to go."

"Shut up," Lindsey says.

"All I'm saying is *karma* isn't just a five-letter word."

Lindsey glares at her. "What is wrong with you? Do you think we should give up?"

"I think it's pretty clear there isn't much chance," Lauren says.

"Look," I say, "let's just worry about getting out of here. That's going to be hard enough."

I look at Lauren, and she sighs.

"I can get food," she says.

"I'll go through the clothes," Lindsey says. "Pack things for us."

"We need some place to store stuff," I say.

"There's that hall closet on our floor," Michael says. "No one uses it. I don't think they'll look in there. If we're going to go pretty quickly, I mean."

I can see they feel like I do; they're scared but excited, too. We are going to act. For the first time since they conquered us, we're going to do something unexpected. We're going to fight back. Sure, we're going to run away to do it, but we're going to fight back.

(((((24)))))

LORD VERTENOMOUS

My dearest,

I am pleased that you and the girls are so close. I can't tell you how glad I will be to have you here.

My father has asked me to send his best wishes to you. He will not visit the colony as planned, though it has been named in his honor. Apparently he has business in another sector. That is what he says publicly. I know better. It's the rumors of our troubles that keep him away. He has ignored my reassurances and canceled his trip to the colony. Once again he allows politics to guide him, and I am left to guide myself. So be it. I don't need him.

My abilities have increased since last we were together. I am much stronger. I am stronger than all of the Handlers now. I have finally matured, and like my father and his father before him, I am reaping the genetic advantage of my bloodline.

I long to see you, to feel you, to link our minds. I think of the beauty of your skin, of the way the green deepens under the hint of blue, and I feel the lack of you deep inside me.

We will be happy here. We will be like royalty. This planet will be our kingdom. I will rule, and you will rule by my side.

Personal Log:

My wife will have heard the rumors by now, too, and will be frightened. I hope my letter will quell her fears. I want her to be happy here. We will be happy.

What is wrong with us Sanginians? Are we not the most powerful beings in the universe? Do we not inspire shock and awe wherever we go? The problem here is a small force of rebels. They are a nuisance, not a threat. The cowardly whispers that the colony will fail undermine us at every turn.

Of course, privately, I too am surprised by the abilities of the rebels to elude and attack us. This should not happen. I blame the scouts. Had they given us accurate information I would have taken more precautions with the product, been more forceful.

But I will not allow failure. Failure is not an option. I will destroy what needs to be destroyed and keep what can be sold. This product has no fatal flaw. The product is willful, yes, but we have had willful slaves in the past.

We will prevail over our enemies and their whisper campaigns against us. I will prevail.

Lauren steals some food, and bottled water. She's made lists of things we might need. She's the kind of girl who makes lists.

Lindsey gets us "outfits" for hot and cool weather. She actually picks clothing to go with our eyes and skin tone and hair color. She's practically filled the closet with clothes.

"It's not that I have anything against being the best dressed escapee in history, but we don't have room for all that stuff," I say to Michael.

He says, "When the time comes, we'll just grab a bag of essentials."

That night at dinner, we try to talk down the aliens' power in order to give ourselves courage.

"No alien is going to catch me," Michael says.

"I'd like to see them catch me," Lindsey says. "I will kick some alien butt if they do."

That makes Michael smile. Lust will do that. It can make crazy look cute.

"I know I've been able to hide things from them," I say.

"Me too," Lauren says.

"They aren't as strong as they think they are," I say.

"Not nearly," Lauren says.

"They can't catch us," Michael says.

Then we lapse into silence.

"So we're ready," Lauren says, breaking it.

"Except that we don't know how to get past the security traps and whatever else is out there," I say.

"What security traps?" Lauren says.

"I've been meeting a girl in a dream," I say. "She told me about them."

This pretty much stops conversation. Everyone is looking at me. They're waiting. When you go through an alien invasion, your perspective kind of changes. I can feel their skepticism, but I feel something else, too.

"She's his dream girl," Michael says.

"Dream girl?" Lauren raises her eyebrows. They practically form disapproving question marks.

"She's not my dream girl," I say. "I communicate with her in a dream. That's not the same thing."

"Of course not," Michel says, winking at Lindsey.

She laughs. Lindsey says, "Is this some kind of joke?"

"No," I say.

It's strange, but I can feel that they all kind of believe me.

"So where is she?" Lauren asks.

"Locked in a room."

"Why?"

"I don't know."

"Probably that's where they keep dream girls," Michael says.

Lindsey and Michael actually high-five each other. I really wish they hadn't gotten together.

"She knows things," I say.

"What kind of things?"

"She knows about the rebels. She seems to know about the aliens."

"How?"

"I don't know."

"Doesn't that worry you?" Lauren says. "It worries me."

"She's like us, but she knows more and we need her."

"I don't like this. She's locked away by herself. She

comes to you in a dream. We don't know anything about her."

"It doesn't matter," I say. "What matters is that we don't know enough."

"Enough?" Lindsey says. "What are you talking about?"

"We don't know enough to get out of here alive," I say. "If she can give us some edge we need her."

"Maybe," Lauren says.

"I say get her," Lindsey says. "We're going to need all the help we can get."

"Dream girl," Michael says. "Talking to a girl in dreams. We're all freaks, Tex, but you are freak squared."

Lindsey giggles. I think for a moment they're going to high-five each other again, but I'm saved from that when Lauren says, "I trust you, Jesse. If you say we need her, then I guess we do."

Everyone starts eating again. We're scared. We're excited. A Handler passes close by. I can feel his power more now that I'm stronger. We all can. For a few seconds the air buzzes as if it's full of bees. We keep eating, but the excitement is gone. The fear, though—it stays.

(((((**26**)))))

LORD VERTENOMOUS

To Senator & High Lord Vertenomous:

I am aware of the delicacy of your situation. I understand the political ramifications of a scandal. We still don't have any proof that they are aware or even capable of hearing without our help. If you could allow me to conclude my investigation before making the transfer, I can ensure the success of the colony.

To Senator & High Lord Vertenomous:

Yes, I have received the official inquiry from the Coalition of Species Rights and other inquiries from religious sources who claim to be concerned that this product may be capable of linking to the One. If those fanatics had their way, we would still be struggling to survive in our dying solar system or we would be extinct. I know how you feel about them. I know you agree with me. If we just put them off and keep them away from the planet, all will be fine. The number of product that can hear on this planet is very small. An insignificant number. I admit they may have some latent ability that we have awakened, but it is far from awareness.

I understand the pressures you are under and I appreciate your help. I will not disappoint you.

To Senator & High Lord Vertenomous:

We have a problem. I've had my science officer do experiments on the product because we've detected changes, an increase in the abilities of those that could hear from the start and many who have developed hearing since initial contact, roughly ten thousand, perhaps a few more if rumors of rebel camps are true.

My science officer compared it to what happened on Rayden 2, where a similar change occurred. Apparently contact with us stimulated a part of the product's mind that they couldn't access before. What is most important is that the product on Rayden 2 advanced only to the level of a child. Many of them even lost hearing skill after that, but none, not one, advanced further. My science officer anticipates the same will happen here.

Nevertheless, we both know there will be an outcry across the Republic from species rights and religious groups who will claim the product is aware and cannot, by law, be treated as product. The company would suffer significant losses, unacceptable losses.

Here is my proposition: I will destroy all hearing product on this planet. The other heads of houses have already been contacted and all have agreed to my plan. We will claim that the product that could initially hear lost the ability. You will send me a small number of hearing product from our holdings to compensate for my loss. We'll begin a campaign immediately to undermine the inevitable accusations. With quick, decisive action, we can still make this a profitable acquisition. The company will, no doubt, be very grateful.

We practice talking with our minds, and though we can't hear each other perfectly—it's a little like a cell phone with a faulty signal—we can all do it. I try to hear the Handlers talking to one another. Occasionally I hear bits of thoughts.

That night in the library, we all talk to each other with our minds. I can hear everyone pretty clearly except for Lauren. Her voice is lost in static every few seconds. She has to ask what's been said, too, and it frustrates her. She's used to being the quickest at everything.

We're all freaks, Michael thinks. *What is happening to us? We're all turning into freaks. Nothing as freaky as dream boy here, but still.*

Maybe we'll turn back into ourselves when we get away from them, Lindsey thinks.

It won't be like that, I think. *We're all hearing more. I hear other people sometimes now. I bet you do, too.*

Lindsey thinks, *The other day I heard a girl thinking about her mother and aunt. It was like a memory.*

So it's maybe like an evolutionary change, Lauren thinks.

Both Michael and Lindsey groan.

I'm just saying, maybe it's permanent. Evolutionary changes have always caused discomfort.

I think, *Like when apes went one way and what would become humans went another, there were probably hard feelings. There were probably some apes yelling at the ones becoming humans, "You guys are total freaks!"*

Shut up, Michael thinks.

We're preoccupied, and that's why we don't hear Anchise.

You're reading each other.

"What?" I say. "No. Reading? No."

Everyone else denies it.

You're lying.

We start denying it again.

Go to your rooms, he thinks, though we still have

time before we normally have to go to our rooms.

A geeky guy named Ted uses my line about Anchise's biological clock being off. I want to tell him to shut up, but I don't get the chance. Anchise doesn't even look at him. Ted falls to the floor. Ted is dead.

Sorry for your loss, Anchise thinks, not sounding sorry at all.

Anchise tells everyone to go to their rooms, and they all do. They practically run for the stairs. I can feel how he likes this. But something is wrong. They've been careful with us since those first few weeks. We're property. We're valuable. Even Handlers like Anchise have kept themselves from damaging us. Until now. Something has changed.

I try to go to sleep early that night. Of course it takes me a while. I have to count sheepdogs again. I get into the thousands this time.

I dream. I'm beside myself, which strikes me as funny because it was one of my mom's sayings. She would say, "I was beside myself with worry." That's me now, literally. I don't look at myself, though, because it's just too strange.

I go into Michael's dream. How predictable. He's on a football field. He's wearing his football uniform.

A referee sees me and throws a flag. "Delay of game!" he shouts.

I leave. I was going to see if I could take Michael with me to Catlin's, but I change my mind. I go alone. Catlin is standing by her window.

"They're coming," she says.

(((((28)))))

LORD VERTENOMOUS

Personal Log:

Anchise reported that the slaves were reading each other in the library. They were having a conversation. Couldn't this be a good thing, though? Product that evolves because of us and can do advanced work. We could have a new class of slave. A better one. We could breed them.

But those in power have no vision.

We have our plan. We will create a net, each of us taking a point, and we will close around them, extinguishing their faint flames. It will be quick and painless, but what a waste. I am truly sorry.

(((((29)))))

"Who's coming?" I say. But even as I say it, I hear them. I hear them gathering. It's not exactly gathering, though, because they're in different places. I'm confused. They're together but not together.

"They're joining," she says.

"They're what?"

"They're going to kill us."

"I'll be back," I say.

"Don't leave me," she cries. But I do.

I go back to my room, but then I can't wake myself. I stand there beside myself, the fear pounding in me, and I can't wake up. Then my mother comes to me. She's standing over me like she did so many times when she woke me for school. "Time to wake up, Jess." It's like it's really her, like she's back. I am so happy for a second. Then I wake up. The sorrow and fear hit me at the same moment. I jump up from the floor.

"They're going to kill us!" I shout. "Run!"

Everyone wakes up pretty quickly. No one needs an explanation of who "they" are. No one doubts that they will kill us, either. We all run out into the hall, and things get chaotic.

"They're close," I say to Michael. "You get Lindsey and Lauren. I've got to get Catlin."

We both run up the stairs. I know Catlin's room is up high. I know that much. But when we get to the girls' floor, I'm confused. There's nowhere else to go, no fourth floor, no attic that I can see.

Catlin, I shout with my mind. *Catlin.*

I hear something. It's a faint voice. A lot of people are waking now and there's fear everywhere, like something sharp and cold in the air, like a stinging rain, but I hear Catlin calling my name. I know she's shouting, but to me it's barely a whisper.

She's on this floor. I meet Lauren and Lindsey and Michael coming out of the girls' room.

"You go get the supplies," I say. "I'll meet you outside the kitchen door."

Lauren hesitates.

"Go," I say.

And she does. They all do. I listen. Everything is chaos around me. People screaming, pushing, shoving.

I stand still. I make my mind find silence and I hear her more clearly, and then it appears at the end of the hall: a door.

"Jesse," she shouts. "Jesse."

"I'm here," I say.

"Where?"

"Outside. There's a door."

"Of course," she says. "The tower is an illusion. He made it all up. It's just a room, isn't it?"

"It's just a room. What should I do?"

"I don't know," she says. "Do something. Try something."

So I try opening the door and it opens right up. I try walking through it, but as soon as I get in the doorway, it feels like this one time that I was stupid enough to touch an electric fence, but worse. I'm thrown back on my butt, and my whole body is shaking.

I can see the room. I can see Catlin. But she's on the other side of the force field, or whatever it is.

"What did you do?" she says.

"I opened the door. Something stopped me from getting in."

"I told you it's like some kind of spell."

"I can see you," I say.

"Do something."

I stand up. It hurts. My feet feel numb. I force myself to move.

"I don't know what to do."

"Maybe see if you can make the spell look like something you know," she says. "Like a curtain maybe. Then try to tear it."

I hear something that sounds like water rushing toward me. It's loud. It sounds like a killer wave. I suddenly slip back into a memory, only it seems more real than a memory: I'm a kid and we're white-water-rafting in Colorado and I fall out of the raft. I get caught on a rock and I'm pounded by rushing water and then pulled under. I can't do anything. I know I'm going to die. Then I'm out of the water. My dad has me somehow. He's saying my name over and over.

No.

"It's not real," I say out loud. I know my dad isn't here to save me.

I concentrate on seeing a curtain in front of me.

"Are you doing it?" she says.

"I'm trying."

"Me too," she says. "I'm trying, too."

"I'm pulling at it."

"Wait, look at the bottom."

I see it. A tear. I yank it. I hear the rushing water behind me. I feel the memory of being pulled under the water, being held there, and being sure I'd never get back to the surface. "But you did get back to the surface," my father's voice says. "You got back."

I yank a big piece off the curtain.

"We're getting it," she says.

We're pulling and yanking and finally it unravels and Catlin runs out of the room. She runs right past me.

"Come on," she says. "There's no time."

It's hard getting down the stairs. They're jammed with people. About halfway down, we jump over the rail. It's about an eight-foot drop, but it would take too long to shove our way through the crowd. I lead Catlin to the kitchen. It's easy to get there. Everyone else is going the other way, trying to get out the doors in the den and front. We step out the back door. I hear a few voices at the front of the house, but I also hear people screaming inside that the doors are locked.

Lauren, Michael, Lindsey! I shout with my mind.

They shout back. They're close. I see them down past the pool. No one else is there.

"Come on," I say to Catlin.

The three of them are staring at something. Then I see it. A wall. Not the stone wall that surrounds the grounds but something much taller and wider. At first it looks like some kind of metal. Then it becomes a mirror and I can see our reflections in it. I can see the house, and because the lights are on, I can see faces up against the windows in the den. I can hear windows break but no one gets out. Something is holding them in. I hear them screaming.

"This is why there weren't any traps," Catlin says. "They've put everything into this wall. They're going to destroy everyone inside it."

"But we're valuable," Lauren says.

"They don't care anymore."

The wall is enormous. I see in my mind that it stretches to the sky and into the earth, that it is as deep as a city block. To me it now becomes steel. It's the worst thing I could imagine. Am I imagining it? How else is it possible for it to keep changing?

"It's not real," I say.

"It's real," Catlin says.

"What we see isn't. It's like what he did to trap you in your room, only more powerful. What do you see it as?"

"It's like a mountain," she says. "It's like a smooth cliff. Black and shiny."

I hear the wall of water crash over the house and I know it's only a matter of minutes before it will bury me. Bury us.

Michael takes a run at the wall. I know he thinks he can break through it like he broke through the tackles of three-hundred-pound linemen. He bounces off it.

Lindsey says we need to climb it. We'll never break

through something so thick. She thinks of the wall as stone. She starts to climb it, but she's not really climbing. She only thinks she is.

"Follow me," she says. "Come on, we can go over it."

Lauren sees her climbing, sees her climbing right up a rock wall, and starts doing the same. They're both caught in the same illusion. They're not climbing anything. I can tell that Michael sees this, but he wants to believe that they're escaping. He's trying to convince himself that he should climb, too. I grab Lindsey and pull her back, and the illusion breaks. Lauren falls.

"It keeps changing," Catlin says. "It becomes what we think it is."

Lauren looks angry. She stands. "It fools us into thinking we've found a way out. That's how it keeps us in."

"Find the weakness," I say. "The curtain had a weak spot. Maybe this thing does, too."

I hear people in the house screaming. A thousand screams. They're drowning. They're being buried in water. I guess that's probably an illusion, too, but it's an illusion that's killing people. I hear death.

Michael hits the wall. He's hitting it with his fist, but his mind is hitting it at the same time. His hand starts to bleed. He grimaces, but he keeps hitting. Something does break. A piece, I think.

The wall becomes glass then. That's what I see. It looks like I could shatter it with a palm-heel strike. I show Michael the strike so that he doesn't break his hand hitting the wall with his fist, and I tell him to strike where I do. We stand side by side and strike it. The glass makes a sound but doesn't shatter. I take a few steps back and do a sliding side kick. Then a back kick. I'm trying to make each of these physical movements a mental one, too. I'm trying to force my mind to strike against the wall.

I stop.

"Don't stop," Michael says. "We're getting it."

"It's letting us think we're getting it."

Catlin takes my hand. I turn and see she's grabbed Lauren's hand, too.

"Hold hands," she shouts.

I've been distracted by the wall, but now I hear the water only a few feet behind us. It's a roar. I feel it pulling me under.

Everybody is holding hands.

"You've got to think of us all together."

I feel Michael and Lindsey pulling away when she says this.

"Do it!" I yell. "Just do it. Now."

"Run at the wall," Catlin says.

I see it then. See what we've got to do. *See us punching through it. All of us,* I think to the others.

For a moment our minds join. We run at the wall.

Then I hear the aliens. *We're very sorry for your loss.*

«««((30))))»»

The wave passes. A part of it comes through the hole and knocks us all on our butts; we're lucky, though: the wall holds most of it in. When it's past, I hear silence behind it. No screaming now, just dead silence.

"We've got to get going," I say.

We help each other up. We all know that we were meant to be part of that silence and it won't take them long to realize we aren't. The most powerful beings in the universe will not be happy.

"Get going where?" Lindsey says.

"Find a car, something that we can use to get away and out into the country."

We run. The bushes and tree leaves are wet, and before long we're soaked. We hit a patch of thorn bushes so then we're soaked *and* cut up. We keep looking back, expecting the Handlers to swoop down on us at any minute. A few times I think I even hear the rush of water, but it's just my imagination. We're all breathing hard but we keep running like our lives depend on it because they do.

"Break," Lindsey calls.

I don't stop.

"Come on," Lauren says.

I stop.

"Where are you taking us?" Lindsey says through heavy, short breaths.

"The city."

"This is the best way?" Lauren says. She's trying to slow her breathing. She has her hands pressed together in front of her. I hear her trying to think yoga thoughts, trying to slow her racing heart.

"More like the best way to hell," Lindsey says.

"You want to lead?"

"I doubt I could do any worse."

She doesn't say anything more, though.

"We need to keep moving," I say.

We run some more. Then we come to a bridge and downtown is in front of us. We take a second rest. We're all sucking air now.

"Is there water?" I ask.

Lauren shakes her head. "We couldn't get to the food or clothes. It was just too crazy in there."

"Think they know we're gone yet?" Michael says.

"He'll know," Catlin says.

We don't need to ask who he is.

"Wonder if there are any cars left," Michael says.

This worries me a little. They were destroying every machine they could find when we worked downtown, including a lot of cars. But they used trucks and buses, so they didn't destroy those. I don't see us escaping in a Greyhound, though.

"We've got to get out somehow," I say. "It will just get harder the longer we're here."

"Maybe not," Lauren says. We all look at her. "Addyen showed me her house. In my mind, I mean. It's in a neighborhood called Hyde Park."

"I know that neighborhood," I say. "It's north of the university. My uncle lived there."

"Her house is on Avenue B."

"So what?" Lindsey says.

"She'll help us," Lauren replies. "She thinks it's wrong that we're slaves. She'll help us escape."

I think about this and about Addyen giving us dessert that night, and I think we don't have anywhere else to go. "Let's do it."

"We all need to agree," Michael says. "It's all of our lives at risk here."

So we vote, and we all agree that it's the best choice of bad choices.

Lauren turns to Catlin. "But before we go to Addyen's house, I want some answers, like how you know so much about the aliens."

Catlin doesn't say anything. "I don't know if I trust her," Lauren says.

"But you trust me, right?" I say.

Lauren looks at me like she's not sure, but she says, "Okay, Jesse. For now." We hurry on. We make it to downtown, which has been seriously transformed. Even with the dim lamps that light the path, we can see that. They've torn down some buildings, but the big change is that all the streets are gone and have been replaced by either grass or wide pebble walkways. Somehow they've already got leafy trees and thick bushes everywhere. As I'm taking all this in, I hear a ship overhead, one of those little ships that buzz around about forty feet off the ground.

Not one ship but two come into sight behind us. I hear alien minds scanning the area. I think they're using some kind of echo device in the ships to help them. They've followed our trail.

"Get down," Lauren says.

"There's no place to hide, genius," Lindsey says. "They'll hear us even if we're in the bushes."

"She's right," Michael says. "They'll know we're here."

Lauren is used to giving orders, but I can see she's uncertain now. "Hiding in the bushes is better than not hiding at all."

"Oh, please," Lindsey says. "We might as well give them the finger. In fact, that's a good idea." Lindsey illustrates.

"I saw him do something once," Catlin says. "I think it was a way to hide."

"Hide how?" I say.

The others are arguing about getting down or not getting down or who is giving orders. I'm the only one listening to Catlin.

"He made himself fade."

"Listen," I say to the others. I have to say it again and louder, *"Listen."*

They turn toward me with the kind of look I used to give my mom when she shook me awake in the morning.

"Listen to her," I say.

"Get close," Catlin says. I move toward her, and Lauren comes in between Catlin and me and then Michael and Lindsey come closer, too.

"Try thinking of yourself as light," Catlin says, "as light as a feather, as light as air. Think of yourself as so light that you're not really here."

"What is she talking about?" Lindsey says.

"Do it," I say.

And, surprisingly, they all do. They all try, anyway. I feel pretty stupid. I feel like a kid playing at being invisible. One of the ships is almost above us.

My arm disappears and Catlin's head disappears. Then I look down and see one of my legs disappear, too, and Catlin disappears almost entirely. I can still see her, but she's vague.

The others are trying, but they're still visible.

"Think of yourself as thin," I say, because that's what I did. "Then think of yourself as so thin you aren't here."

"I am thin," Lindsey snaps.

"Just do it," Lauren says.

Lauren fades a little and so does Michael, but Lindsey doesn't.

"Not so thin now," Lauren says to Lindsey.

"You're not much better."

They get a little better then, competing, but not like Catlin and me. The ship is close. Lindsey is the most visible, so I put my arms around her. I see Catlin doing the same with Lauren, and Lauren fades more and Catlin shows slightly more. But together that way, they're less visible. The ship passes over us and beyond. After a few minutes, I let Lindsey go.

"We're definitely freaks," she says.

"Yeah," I say, "but you have to admit that was kind of cool."

There are things about these new powers that I like. If it weren't for the complete destruction of our planet and the enslavement of our species, I might even think these powers could be a good thing.

"You think you can find the neighborhood from here?" Lauren asks me.

"I think so."

We walk through downtown.

"Look at this," Lindsey says. "Look what they've done. They can't have done this to New York City. No way. I bet New York fought them off. New Yorkers would know how to deal with aliens."

"No one fought them off," Lauren says.

No one else says anything. What can we say? What do we really know? But the thing is, I do know. New York is no different from anyplace else; New York belongs to them now.

«««((**31**))»»»

LORD VERTENOMOUS

Personal Log:

It is impossible that slaves, that product, could create a hole in the boundary, so when a Handler reported this, I could only think that we who were joined did it. Some surge of power we couldn't control must have made a hole. It is an unlikely explanation, but far more unlikely is the possibility that slaves could break through my boundary.

I ordered inventory done immediately. It is possible that some of the slaves escaped. Doubtful but not outside of the realm of possibility. Reports of successful product destruction have come in from the other heads of houses across the colony. These reports were inter-rupted by Anchise, who did a sweep of the house and grounds. He claimed some of our product is missing.

Check again, I ordered.

I've checked twice, lord.

He showed me who's missing, and one of them is my second, Catlin. For a moment I suspect she learned something from me that helped her escape, but what could she have learned? It's absurd. It's as absurd as product breaking through my boundary. I can only think that they were running and they came to the wall just as we who were joined made a hole. They were lucky enough to be nearby, and they jumped through the hole as we swept over the grounds. It is an unfortunate coincidence.

Find them, I ordered. *And take another Handler with you.*

Another?

Take another.

Anchise could not conceal his anger, but I will not underestimate this product again.

I will destroy them, he told me. Not a question.

Yes. But then I changed my mind. *No. Bring them back. Broken is fine but if you can, bring them. We will take them apart and see what they have become.*

They will be broken. Anchise cannot control his anger. This troubles me because these are slaves. We should feel nothing for them, but I understand his feeling; they have caused us much uneasiness. I bang my fist on the table. This species was so easy to defeat. How has it become so difficult and so complicated when at first it was so very easy?

I don't want to think it, but it just sort of pops into my head. *I like what they've done to the place.* That's wrong on so many levels, but I have to admit that their downtown is more attractive than the old one of concrete and cramped spaces and stone and metal buildings.

There are lots of bushes and trees that I don't recognize, all shades of blue or green. Aqua and turquoise. We pass a tall aqua tree with leaves as big as dinner plates, and it's amazing. Totally amazing. It's like being on another world.

I say, "It's kind of beautiful." I know I should hate anything that belongs to them, that comes from them. But, this power we have, a gift, comes from them.

As soon as I say *beautiful,* Michael gives me a look like I've just said something Benedict Arnold or Brutus would say.

"I wish we could burn it all down," Lindsey says.

"Sure," I say guiltily. "Me too, but—"

"But you're right," Lauren says. "It is kind of beautiful. They won't be cutting down rain forests. They aren't going to have machines that fill the air with pollution."

"I can't believe you," Lindsey says. "Are you listening to yourself?"

"I'm just saying that from an ecological standpoint, the world's in better hands."

"You sound like you're glad they're here," Lindsey says.

"Not me," Lauren says. "Maybe Mother Earth is."

"Not me, either," I say. "I'd send them all back where they came from. All we're saying is the green is nice."

"I hate it," Lindsey says.

"I hate it, too," Catlin says bitterly. "They think they can do anything they want to us. They think it's their world. I'd destroy it all."

Lindsey nods. "That's right, girl. Destroy it all. Destroy them."

It's not that I don't feel the same way. I'll think of my parents and feel it. I'll think of my friends, my dog. Sometimes I feel nothing but hate. But if I don't fight that feeling, I start to hate myself, too. I survived. I survived because some part of me is a little like them.

"It's starting to get light," I say. "We should hurry. We need to be there before dawn."

We're all tired, but we force ourselves to keep going. We try to keep to cover. We see the ships again; they're off to our right making a pass back toward Lord Vert's mansion. We see them two more times, farther and farther off to the right.

We get beyond downtown and cross the University of Texas campus. North of that is a narrow little park and a neighborhood with spacious, older homes. Comfortable but not pretentious. We're almost to the end of the park when we run into the alien.

As we get closer to him, I feel dizzy. I stumble. My mind becomes fuzzy. I can't see as well. This alien is a little larger than most of them, but not as large as a Handler.

Good evening, he thinks, slurring the word *evening.* He's not speaking out loud, but I feel his voice unable to enunciate, and I realize he's drunk. *How unexpected.*

He sounds amused. I look at the others to see if they are feeling what I'm feeling, but I can't tell. No one moves.

Four slaves out on an errand.

Is he making us drunk on purpose or are we susceptible to his drunkenness? I've never seen a drunk alien before. Then I think, *Four slaves?* I look around. Catlin's gone.

"You're right," I say, "for Lord Vert. We're delivering a message for the lord."

The alien smiles. *Lord Vert? Wonderful. I must remember that. Lord Vert. Not wise to tell anyone who might let it get back to him. Don't have to worry about me, humans. Not likely he and I will ever cross paths. No, not likely at all.*

Michael moves to the alien's right, but he stumbles as he does. I'm pretty sure then that the alien is somehow making us drunk on purpose; I can feel him pushing his own drunkenness onto us, almost like it's a cloud he's emitting.

I'm impressed. I was told this planet had no hearing. You certainly do hear, don't you?

I can't see Catlin, but I feel her on the other side of the alien. He turns and waves his arm, and she reappears. *Impressive.*

He looks around at each of us. *You have nothing to fear from me. I am here illegally. I have no interest in runaway slaves, and if I draw attention to myself, I will end up, well, let's just say in a place I would very much prefer to avoid.*

"What do you mean, here illegally?" I say.

I'm a trader.

"In slaves?" Michael says.

I feel myself moving one way and the other. It's like we're on a ship. The ground is not steady.

I trade in just about everything but slaves. On a new colony there are many opportunities. I have my own ship and I pay the right people and I'm able to make deals now, in the early days.

"You're a smuggler?"

The alien smiles. *I prefer* trader. *Give my best to Lord Vert when you see him.*

As soon as the alien is about fifteen feet away, I start feeling less dizzy. He stops at the end of the block. *This may be of little help to you, but I never cared much for slavery. We plan to settle here, but that is not inevitable. New worlds are always being made available to us. It's a big universe. If we don't like what we see, some of us might keep going. That's why the company can't let you live. Don't ever think they've given up on killing you.*

He walks off shaking his head and thinking *Lord Vert.*

We walk in a different direction. Silent. We know he's right. They won't give up.

Before we've gone far, the sun slips above the horizon. The air lightens and I feel exposed. I'm walking next to Lindsey, who looks exhausted, and I hear her thinking of herself in the third person, which is bizarre. *Lindsey does not even camp. Lindsey does not do desert. Lindsey's white skin does not get exposed to the aging rays of a frickin' desert sun.*

"Stay out of my head," she says when she notices me reading her.

"Sorry."

We cross 38th Street on Speedway. I think we're in Hyde Park and I think Speedway is a main road, but I don't know if Avenue B is to the right or left of us. I choose the wrong direction because we hit Avenue F, then G. We're all exhausted, and this mistake seems larger than itself, like a sign of failures to come. We turn around and go back, all aware that we're out in the open, that we would be easy to spot.

Then I see a light come on in a house and my emotions swing the other way. For a second an irrational hope spikes in me: others survived. But then I realize it's not people in that house or in any of the other houses. The alien settlers have moved in.

We get onto Avenue B and go north. This time we make the right choice. Lauren sees the house at the end of the next block. Another light comes on in a house we're passing, and we make a run for it. It's a flat-out sprint. Michael beats us to the door. He's fast. He's always said he's fast, but I didn't realize how fast.

This house is like a lot of houses in the neighborhood. Older. Small. Nothing has been changed yet. The houses haven't even been painted green.

I bang on the door, louder than I mean to.

"Easy, dude," Michael says.

But I don't want to be easy. I bang again. They're in our houses. They're in our homes. They aren't our houses. We have no homes.

I feel Addyen. She doesn't come to the door physically, but her mind scans us. Her surprise quickly becomes fear, a fear that fills her house.

Addyen, Lauren thinks. *Let us in.*

I was very foolish.

You told me you wanted to help, Lauren thinks. *We need your help now.*

I was foolish.

They were going to kill us.

You shouldn't have come here.

We're here, I interrupt. *Someone is going to see us if you don't open the door.*

A second later she opens the shield that's around the house. I think it's like what Lord Vert made but much weaker.

Inside, Addyen has already painted the rooms various shades of green. The furniture looks like it was in the house before, even the books in the bookcases. Maybe they'll replace these later, but now it looks like she's stolen the life of whoever lived in the house.

I do not know you, she thinks to Catlin.

"I'm Catlin."

She's bothered by Catlin. I feel that. She pushes her way into Catlin's mind. At first Catlin blocks her, but Addyen does something and Catlin can't keep her out. She blushes, and Addyen looks away.

I'm sorry, she thinks.

Lauren looks at Catlin, who is careful not to look back.

Although Addyen is anxious, the initial spike of fear has eased. *You must be hungry. I will make you some food.*

I don't think I'm hungry when she says this, but when Addyen puts out the food, all of us go at it as if we haven't eaten in days. Well, all of us except Lindsey.

"Just eat," Lauren tells her. "You don't know when we'll get the chance to eat again."

"Mind your own business," Lindsey says, but she does eat a little then.

"This is great," Michael says to Addyen.

Addyen, who has been quiet until now, asks what happened at the mansion. We tell her.

"They're all dead," Catlin says. "No one could survive that."

Addyen says what they always say: *I'm sorry for your loss.*

"Don't say that," I say.

But I am.

"You're killing us."

"She's not killing us," Lauren says, putting her hand on my arm.

"Her kind."

"But not her."

What has happened is wrong, Addyen thinks. *You are connected to the One. You should not be killed, and you should not be treated like product. There are many in the Republic who would feel as I do. It would cause many, many problems for the developers of this planet.*

"Like what?"

Many problems. If we had known before, we would not have come. We settle only where the lead species is primitive.

"But you came," I say. "You're here. So what now?"

Addyen says she doesn't know, but I think she does. She says we must stay in the house. Her husband is landing in an hour and he will know what to do. *He is a good man. He will help you.*

I consider telling her that we want to escape to the west, but I don't. I'm worried about her husband. Maybe he won't feel as sympathetic to escaped slaves. Maybe he won't want us here.

««««(((33)))»»»»

About thirty minutes later, Addyen says she needs to meet her husband.

"How can we trust you?" I say.

I will not report you. I must meet him. I have said I would. If I don't, he will worry. Perhaps he will ask someone to check on me.

I'm worried. We all are, but in the end it seems better to let her go. Will she come back with her husband or with Handlers ready to end us with an apology? We all sit around waiting for the answer to that. We don't talk much.

About two hours pass before Addyen and her fat husband come through the doorway. He does not look pleased to see us. He turns to Addyen. *What have you done? Lord Vertenomous has declared this product runaways.*

"We aren't anyone's product," Michael says.

You see, Addyen's husband thinks, as if Michael has just confirmed a point he's been trying to make. *You see what happens? They get ideas.*

Michael stands. "We get ideas? You know what? We're your equals. If you fought fair, you'd see we're more than your equals."

Addyen's husband acts like he hasn't heard Michael. I have to admit that Michael sounds like a kid on a playground.

Addyen's husband thinks to her, *They will get us terminated.*

"What's he talking about?" Lauren asks Addyen.

Addyen is silent, so her husband tells us. *Runaways will be terminated. It is the law. Anyone who helps runaways faces the same penalty. If they find you here, we will die, too. You have to leave at once.*

None of us move. I'm sorry to have put Addyen in this position, but I'm not sorry enough to leave. It's light out there. Aliens are all around.

"I guess you better make sure no one finds us then," Lindsey says.

"Yeah," Michael says, "'cause we're not leaving."

I think Addyen's husband considers killing us.

Let's all calm down, Addyen interrupts. *Bathamous is not going to inform on anyone or force anyone to leave. I will make us drinks, and we will find a solution.*

None of us really believes the part about a solution, but we pretend we do.

Bathamous follows Addyen into the kitchen.

We listen to them. Though Addyen knows we can hear, she underestimates our ability.

They cannot allow them to live now, Bathamous argues. *They will lose profits.*

We can get word out. There will be outrage.

But it will come later. It will come after the product has been destroyed. What good will it do then? What good will it do them or us?

It's wrong, she thinks. *It's wrong to slaughter them. They are not product.*

They are savages. They slaughtered each other. I've been reading about them on the voyage. They have been destroying each other and the green and blue of their world for a long time. They would have destroyed themselves without us. Or if they managed to survive each other, their machines would have conquered them. The One has not chosen them.

They are not product, Addyen thinks stubbornly.

When they come back to the living room, I say, "What would happen to us if you can convince your leaders we aren't product? What would happen if we can stay alive long enough?"

You can't, Bathamous thinks. *Your pictures are in the minds of every person here in Lord Vertenomous's capital. A million Sanginians disembarked here this morning.*

"But if we could," I say. "Stay alive. If we could, what would happen to us?"

Perhaps, Addyen thinks, *there would be land set aside for you. A small bit of land for you to survive and live out your time. One of your islands. Something remote.*

That is a dream, Bathamous thinks.

"Like a reservation?" Lauren says.

Addyen doesn't reply, but we know the answer. And I know that whatever the high-minded among their species wish for us, we cannot survive colonization. They might regret what has happened here, but most will shrug and say it was inevitable, just as Addyen's husband is doing now.

Addyen passes around the drink. It tastes like motor oil, but we all try to take a few sips. When Addyen goes to make more for her husband and herself, Bathamous thinks, *You are not product. I am sorry you will all be killed, but there is no other way. It has gone too far.*

Like all Sans, he's polite.

(((((34)))))

We go out into the backyard to get away from Addyen and her husband. The yard has a fence around it, so we hope we'll be unnoticed. We're all shaken by his pronouncement. Lindsey says she wishes she had a cigarette.

"You smoke?" Michael says.

"You think it might kill me? I had to quit when they invaded and I ran out of cigarettes. I don't know which was worse."

"So what do we do now?" Lauren says, looking at me.

They're all looking at me.

"We can't stay here. We can't trust Bathamous. We can't even, you know, tie him up or something. He'd make it a fight. We can't risk that."

"I say we go to New York City," Lindsey says. "That's the one place we might have a chance to fight."

"It's a long way," Michael says.

"Do you want to hide or fight?"

She's appealing to Michael's macho side.

"How would we get there?" Lauren says.

"Same way we'd get anywhere," Lindsey says.

We all kind of smile at this. We have no way to get anywhere, so I guess we could say we were going to the North Pole and it wouldn't be all that less likely.

"There are rebels out West," I say.

"We don't know that."

"I do," Catlin says. She's been standing off to the side a little. She comes and stands next to me. "I know they attacked and killed a patrol. They're out there. I feel they're out there."

"I feel it, too." I remember my dream. I try not to think of the threatening presence that was in the square with them. I try just to believe in the rebels. "They're in Taos or near Taos," I say.

She nods.

"Okay," Lindsey says. "They're out there. You're probably right, but there are probably rebels in other places, too. There will be rebels in New York, and we'll be able to find them."

"Let's vote, then," I say.

"Vote?" she says. "I know how it will go. The girls will side with you and Michael will side with me."

"It's not about you or him," Michael says. "It's about what we should do to stay alive."

"Fine," she says. "Let's vote."

She's wrong about the vote. Michael doesn't vote with her. She smiles. "Fine," she says. "That's just great." She walks back toward the house just as Bathamous and Addyen come out. She pushes past them.

We must leave, Addyen thinks. *Bathamous must register.*

"Register?" I say.

He must register. It's the law. All new arrivals must register.

"Why didn't he do it when he got off the ship?" Lauren asks.

It is for the city. You register in your city. You get a ship, some other supplies. All residents must register.

"You get a ship?" I say to Bathamous.

He nods. *Once I'm registered.*

I try to read Bathamous, but I can't. I also can't think of another way we can get out West.

"All right," I say. "Get your ship. Let us borrow it. You can get rid of us, and we can get away."

"No," Michael says. "We can't trust him."

"We need a ship," I say.

"He won't get us a ship," Michael says.

I will get you a ship, Bathamous thinks. *Then I will be rid of you.*

"Okay," Michael says looking at me, "but Addyen stays."

No, Bathamous thinks.

"She stays," Michael says again.

Bathamous looks like he is going to turn Michael off. I've seen that look in Handlers. The others notice too. We spread out around him, not physically but with our minds. It's like at the wall, almost like we're holding hands again, like we're linked somehow with our minds. We do this without thinking. I can feel Bathamous's surprise. Anytime we surprise the aliens, I'm encouraged.

Please, Bathamous, Addyen thinks. *You go.*

No, Bathamous thinks. *Enough. They are above themselves.*

Please.

She doesn't like this, any of it. Not her husband thinking of killing us and not us trying to dictate what she will and won't do. But she tries to make peace.

Her husband sends her a message. It's sudden and very quick. It's like a passing shadow. I can't see the solid part, so I don't have a chance to hear it.

All right, he thinks to us, *I will get you your ship, but you will leave.*

"As soon as it's dark," I say.

LORD VERTENOMOUS

Personal Log:

My wife is resting. After not seeing each other for so long, it is disappointing to argue so soon. We have hardly had time to come together and we are pushing each other away.

The lack of product in the house began the bad feeling. I had promised her sixty and she sees only five and all nonhearing. I promised her that I would bring more slaves in, but she is not satisfied by promises. She has never been in a primitive colony before. She didn't realize how many things she would not have. Already she complains about the lack of nobles with whom to form a society.

Everything depends on good scouting. None of this is my fault. It is the fault of the company and my father's sources, who did not investigate this world the way they should have. Will he take blame? I know better.

The reports on the destruction of product are good but not perfect. Besides my own five runaways, the other houses admit imperfect kills. Still, even accounting for false reports, there can be no more than forty or fifty escaped slaves. If they can be exterminated quickly, all will be well. Sanginians will come and most will not care that there is no hearing product. Most will just see a planet with much green and blue and many fair places to live. They will see opportunity. Yes, it will take the company longer to turn a profit. But I must keep my perspective; in the long run everything will work out.

I was about to write my father and update him and ask again, though I loathed doing it, for hearing product from his nearest colony, when a Handler interrupted me. He had news about the runaways. I ordered him in and he brought with him a short, fat merchant. He was, at least, a citizen of the Republic. I do not like to talk to those who are not. Even so, this meeting seemed a waste of my time. Why did he not simply send a report?

This is Bathamous. He is the husband of your cook. He has seen the runaways.

I was angry.

You have killed them?

He knew why I asked this, because if he saw them and didn't kill them, then both he and his wife would be in violation. Their lives mine, citizens or not.

I could not.

Why is that?

They joined.

Impossible.

Still, it is true.

They are primitives.

Savages, he agreed. *They would have killed me and my wife. They would have tried. I have skills but Addyen is only a cook. With them joined, I could not be sure of the outcome.*

I want to discount this information. I have chosen my Handlers carefully so that we may join when necessary, but it is never easy and it is never comfortable. We cannot stay joined long. We are among the strongest in the empire and it is difficult for us. So I wanted to tell this merchant he was lying or mistaken.

But it is known that species who evolve rapidly, as these have done, whose talents have been ready for many generations, waiting for a spark, sometimes have one special skill. Never has it been one such as joining, and I feel uneasy and angry that it might be possible. I reason that even if true, they are primitives and their joinings are surely primitive. It is more likely this fat merchant exaggerated to save his life.

Where are they? I demanded.

At my house, lord. I made the excuse of registration and came right here. Please, Lord, do not let them harm her. They hold her prisoner.

He lied. He came here, and thought he could lie to me. I broke open his mind to see the truth. I heard him screaming as I did, and I watched him fall to the floor.

I am sorry for your loss.

He believed they joined, Anchise interrupted.

He was mistaken.

Of course, lord.

Kill my cook when you kill the product.

It is the law. Though they are citizens, they have hidden runaways. They have no protection and I have no patience.

Take another, I added.

Again, the Handler's anger was too much to hide. A Handler is a powerful warrior. He is more powerful than a unit of soldiers, more deadly.

I will kill them.

Take another. They escaped you once.

I did not write my father. I did not visit my wife or my daughters. Instead I went up to the room where my second was kept. I looked out her window. I looked around the room. What happened here? What did she learn that is keeping them alive? How did she learn it?

«««(((**36**)))»»»

Michael goes to talk to Lindsey, who is in one of the bedrooms.

Catlin and Lauren and I sit in the living room. I think Lauren's going to start demanding answers from Catlin again. Instead she says, "I'm sorry about what happened to you with Lord Vertenomous."

"I did what I had to do to stay alive," Catlin says.

"There was nothing else you could have done," Lauren says.

"I could have fought him."

"You would have been killed," Lauren says. "Every single person who fought them is dead. How old are you, anyway?"

"Fifteen," Catlin says. Then she looks confused. "Sixteen maybe. I might have just turned sixteen."

Then she begins to cry and maybe it's because of what happened to her and maybe it's because her birthday passed without her knowing. Lauren puts her arm around her, and they stay like that until Addyen comes in.

If you're going to have a ship, she thinks, looking at me, *you will need to fly it.*

"You can show me," I say.

I have a Reader.

"A what?"

It's what we use to get information. There's one back in the bedroom on the left. It is in the closet. It will show you.

"Okay," I say, kind of relieved to leave the room.

As I walk past the bedroom where Michael and Lindsey are, I hear them kissing. I guess she's forgiven him.

I find the Reader right away. I find something else, too, hidden in a shoebox. It's a handgun, a Smith & Wesson .357. I know the aliens are too strong for our weapons, but I take it anyway.

The Reader is easy to use, and it's filled with information. The information doesn't come in words exactly. It feeds directly into my mind in images.

I'm reading about their culture and history. I realize why they hate machines so much now. Machines almost conquered them on their own world, and machines are running a big chunk of the universe. Machines would like to run the Sanginians, too, so they often fight wars. Whenever they get too close to one another, they fight. So far neither has an advantage.

All the Sanginian machines, even something called an echo machine that they used when they invaded Earth, rely on the mental powers of the aliens to make them work. They're different from our machines. We program a computer to do something and it does it. The aliens' machines don't work that way. They have to interact with them.

Lauren comes in and sits on the bed beside me, so close I feel her arm brush mine as she sits. I think she notices, too. I hand her the Reader and I show her articles titled "Earthlings: Their Violent History" and "Best Training Techniques for Primitive Species."

"Weird," she says.

We look at a manual for flying one of their little ships. It doesn't look impossible. They have a basic engine but it's the mind of the driver that makes it work.

"Can you learn how to fly one?" Lauren says.

"I think so," I say. "Maybe. I'll read it over a few times."

She hands the Reader back to me.

We're sitting close together and I remember the kiss she gave me a long time ago, the feel of her hair brushing my cheek.

I'm leaning toward her and she's leaning toward me when the door across the hall swings open and Michael comes out.

"Oh, sorry," he says.

Lauren practically jumps off the bed.

"What did you need?" I say.

"Lauren," he says, a little sheepish. He turns to her. "Lindsey wants you to settle an argument. The girl won't believe me."

"About what?"

He shakes his head. "She thinks Malcolm X was a rap star. I told her who he was, but she won't believe me."

Lauren looks pleased to have the chance to settle an argument.

"Sorry, dude," Michael says as they leave.

I'm disappointed that Lauren and I were interrupted, but then I tell myself I need to focus on keeping us alive, anyway. That's where my mind should be now. I read some more, but I start yawning. Those yawns are hard to overcome after staying up all night. I slip off.

I have a dream. I'm back in our old garage, which my dad had converted into a gym.

"Looks like you're in a tough spot," my dad says, hitting the big bag. He's punching it: a left, right, left, right, hook, combination. Then he steps back for a roundhouse kick and ends with an elbow strike as the bag swings back to him. He stops and looks at me. "Grasshopper."

"Could be worse," I say. "Oh, wait, no it couldn't."

"Could be dead," he points out.

"Are you dead?"

"Can't answer that one," he says. "There are rules."

"We're stronger than we were," I say. "But we're not strong enough."

He nods. "Remember when you used to spar better opponents in tae kwon do?"

I do. I remember being a yellow, green, and blue belt and sparring with black belts. Most of them were too good for me to stay with. They knew too much. They were too fast because the moves came to them without thinking. And they could always anticipate my moves. Well, almost always. Every once in a while, maybe once in a fight, I'd have a chance, an opportunity. That chance usually came from my doing something unexpected.

"It won't be easy," he says.

"You can't tell me if you're alive, if Mom's alive?"

"This is a dream," he says. "How could I know?"

"You really are just a dream?" I was trying to convince myself I'd somehow dreamwalked to a real place and my father was real. The way he looks at me, sad and distant, is my answer.

"You'd better wake up now," he says.

I don't want to leave him, though. I struggle against the urge to open my eyes.

When I do, it's because I hear a sound I've heard before. A ship is landing.

(((((37)))))

I run to the living room. Everyone else is already there. A ship has landed in the yard of the house next door. At first I think it's Bathamous, but he's not in the ship. No one is.

"What are we waiting for?" Lindsey says.

"I thought I heard two ships," I say. Something is wrong. "Where's Bathamous?"

Michael says, "Maybe he's around back."

"We need Addyen," I say.

"You better get her, then," Lindsey snaps.

Lauren runs to the kitchen; in a second she's back.

"Addyen's gone," Lauren says. "No one is in the back."

"No one was watching her?" Lindsey says.

"That's right," Lauren says to Lindsey. "No one was watching her. Not you or Michael, that's for sure."

"This is a trap," I say. "Something's wrong."

Lindsey opens the door. "We've got to make a run for it. We can't just stand here."

"It's going to be tight," I say. "Those patrol ships aren't that big."

"Who's going to fly it?" Michael says.

"It can't be that hard," Lindsey says. "Anyway, they fly close to the ground."

Right, I think. Just like driving a car for the first time. No problem. But really, what else can we do?

We step out onto the front porch. All of us except Lindsey stop there. We all sense that something is wrong. There's at least one Handler here. I feel him. Lindsey keeps walking, seeing only the ship.

"Wait," I say.

"Come on," she says like we're all stupid or slow. She starts to run.

"There's a Handler," I shout.

"Come on, Michael," Lindsey shouts.

"Where is he?" I say to Catlin. "Do you know where he is?"

- "I don't," she says, "but there's another ship, a second Handler."

Then she sends me an image and I see, in my mind, the ship in the backyard two houses up.

"Wait," I shout to Lindsey.

"Michael," Lindsey shouts. "Come on, baby."

She's stopped seeing anything but escape. The ship. Michael. New York. She wants to leave us.

Michael goes after her. I grab for him, but he eludes me like he once eluded all those tacklers.

"You and me, Michael," Lindsey shouts.

"Come on." Michael motions for us to hurry.

Lindsey gets to the ship. It opens. I hear her thinking she's a survivor. I hear her thinking she will survive even if it means leaving the rest of us behind.

Michael hears her, too. He stops in the middle of the yard. He looks back at us.

"They'll get another ship," she says.

He's about to say something, but I will never know what because a Handler appears next to him. Michael raises his arm and lowers his shoulder as if to block a punch. His mind mirrors his physical action. It slows the Handler, but it doesn't stop him. He turns Michael off, and then he turns Lindsey off.

They go silent and still. But the Handler doesn't say it. He doesn't apologize.

We don't have time to pause for even a second. I yank
Catlin and Lauren inside. I reset Addyen's block at the
door. We run for the back, Lauren leading. As we go
down the porch steps into the backyard, I hear the
Handler break through Addyen's block.

Then I realize it isn't the one who killed Michael
and Lauren. It's Anchise.

We loop around the house. There's nowhere to run,
but we run anyway. We run down the street. Anchise
steps out the front door, aware of us, taking his time
now. I think he's smiling.

"Where's the other one?" I ask Catlin.

"He's leaving. He's taking Michael and Lindsey."

"Why would he take them?"

"I don't know."

"Maybe he didn't kill them," I say hopefully. Maybe Michael's block was enough that he survived. The alien wouldn't just carry off the bodies, would he?

We run down the street and I look back and see Anchise step off the lawn and into the street. His mind is like a storm and from that storm comes a wave, like that gigantic and terrifying wave at Lord Vert's. We run but we can't outrun this wave, which is monstrous and moves faster than any person can move. Just like before, I feel the confusion inside me. It scatters my thoughts and I can't concentrate.

Then a bus pulls up next to us; a large, creaky city bus. The door folds open with a cough and a snap.

Get in! Addyen shouts.

She doesn't stop, just slows, and we have to run alongside and jump in through the narrow door. When we're in, she accelerates. Unfortunately we're talking bus, not sports car, so we sputter and cough forward. The bus is no match for the speed of the wave.

You've got to slow it down, Addyen thinks.

The wall of water is twenty feet high. It roars in my ears, and I can feel it trying to pull me back to it.

Catlin is throwing something at it, almost like stones that start to stack together to form a wall but collapse almost immediately.

I get behind Addyen and ask her what we can do to slow it down.

You joined when my husband threatened you. Do it again. Make a wall behind us.

I shout at Catlin that we have to join and make a wall. She says she understands. I say I don't.

"Like this," Catlin says, and tries to show us. It's complicated. I see that we join hands again, join minds, but it's hard to understand the building of the wall.

"We just have to do it," I say. It's like that with kicks and punches and forms. You can only be shown so much. You've got to figure it out for yourself. The only problem is, we don't have time.

I grab Lauren's hand with my left and Catlin's with my right. I feel our minds join and slip away and join and slip away. It's like grabbing hands in a dream and not being able to hold on.

The water washes over the back of the bus but nothing happens, and I realize it won't destroy whatever is in its path. It's more specific than that. It will only destroy us.

"Focus," I shout, as much to myself as to the others. I grab their hands more tightly.

The wall of water inches forward. The confusion is pulling me under. I squeeze the girls' hands and force my mind more deeply into theirs. Lauren groans. Catlin and I are together. Lauren fights to keep her place and she slips again. Then she does it. We're together. Joined.

It starts to happen. We build it together. A wall. Thin at first. Then thicker. Anchise's wall of water rushes forward, and a second later it breaks against our wall, shattering it. I'm knocked to the floor, and I'm pulled away from Lauren and Catlin. They fall, too, Lauren hitting her head on one of the metal poles.

I'm underwater, sinking to the bottom. I can't breathe. It's dark. I'm alone. And I give in to it. I surrender. I let myself sink.

"Going to die are we, Grasshopper?" my dad says.

"I should have died a long time ago," I say. "I should have died when everyone else did."

"Maybe. Maybe we all should have died. No more humans."

"I didn't deserve to survive."

"It's not about deserve, is it? Go ahead and quit. Take the easy way out."

"Shut up. Just shut up." I've never said that to my father.

It's quiet then. I'm sinking in the silence. All alone.

"Dad?"

"I'm here. I'm always here."

"I'm sorry."

"It's not your fault," he says.

"What do I do? How can I go on?"

"Sometimes you have to just put one foot in front of the other."

"That's not going to work underwater."

"It's a metaphor."

"Not a very good one."

"I'm a soldier, not a poet. But you're the last of your kind. We live on in you. In all of you."

I admit then what I've known for a long time. My father is dead. My mother is dead. I'm alive, and if they're alive at all, it's in me.

I fight then. I get mad. I fight my way back to the surface. I force my way through the dark. In a few seconds, I open my eyes, the smell of rotten eggs in the air. I force myself to my feet, the bus bumping and swaying and roaring down the street. Catlin and Lauren are still on the floor of the bus.

The Handler is going to his ship, Addyen thinks. *You slowed his attack enough no one died. But the girls are asleep. I need to wake them before they slip into the deep sleep. Can you drive this thing?*

I slip in behind her as she climbs out. But where do I go? I just floor the stupid thing.

Addyen sends me something in my mind. A map. *Follow.*

At first I don't think I can. I don't see where to

turn, but then I do. I see how her line makes twists and turns through the neighborhood.

Addyen is calling for Lauren, and I realize that she's in Lauren's mind, calling her back from some dark, quiet place. Not sleep but not death, someplace in between. I see Lauren step into the light of her mind, and then it's too bright and I have to look away. Then Addyen goes to Catlin's mind, and the same thing happens and Catlin wakes up, too.

I see Anchise's ship in the rearview mirror. It's closing on us fast now. He'll be over us in a few seconds, and I don't think he'll leave any survivors this time. Addyen nudges me out of the driver's seat and tells me to let her drive again. She tells us to jump as she goes around the next corner. Maybe it will give us a few seconds.

"We'll all jump," Lauren says.

He won't hurt me, Addyen explains. *I'm a citizen. What you felt before wouldn't have hurt me.*

"Please, Addyen."

"Jump," I say, taking hold of Lauren's arm.

We jump and run to the bushes alongside a blue house. The ship passes by a second later, and a second after that the bus explodes.

"Oh, no," Lauren says.

Anchise must realize we aren't on the bus; his ship spins back toward us.

"Take my hands," I tell Lauren and Catlin. "Try to be invisible. You're the best at it, Catlin. Help us."

So we try. We all try. And the ship flies right past us and I think maybe, just maybe, we're good enough together to hide. A few seconds later, it's back, though. It hovers uncertainly and then lands on the front lawn of the house.

(((((39)))))

Anchise gets out of the ship, and I feel him searching with his mind. He's aware of us, but I don't think he can see exactly where we are. He turns to the porch and then to the bushes where we're huddled. He does something and we're not hidden anymore.

I am sorry to have to kill you.

I'm really tired of this absurd apology.

"Maybe I'm not sorry to have to kill you," I say, which sounds kind of crazy, especially since I'm cowering behind a bush.

But it works. Anchise pauses for just a second, wondering if he might have missed something. I go for it then, an elbow shot to his head. That's how I think of it, like a martial arts move, but I'm moving with my mind. He easily blocks it.

Then Lauren does something crazy. She runs at him. She physically runs at him. Catlin throws something between them with her mind, something thorny, which Anchise knocks away. Then he knocks Lauren away and turns to me. By then I've got the gun out of my jeans, the gun I found in Addyen's house. Before Anchise can make his insincere apology, I shoot the son of a female dog in the head. I keep shooting, all head shots.

He falls.

I can hear his confusion. I can hear his disbelief. It's like being killed by a pointed stick. It's an outrage. How is it possible? I keep firing until there are no more bullets and the gun just makes an empty click when I pull the trigger. Catlin has to take the gun from me because I can't stop firing it.

"I am not sorry," I say to a very dead Anchise. "I am not sorry at all."

I kneel down by Lauren. At first I don't think she's breathing, but then I put my finger to her neck and find a pulse. It's soft and erratic, but it's there.

"We need a doctor," I say, but that's a stupid thing to say. No more 911. No more doctors. Anyway, she isn't physically hurt that I can see.

"Lauren," I say.

Then I do the only thing I can do; I go into her mind. It's like walking into fire. I try to back out, but

I'm caught. It's like the fire comes up all around me. I try to calm down. I can't get out of the fire because it's all around me. So I think of what can fight fire. I make water. I make rain. The fire doesn't go out, but it weakens. It weakens enough that I can back out of her mind.

"Let me," Catlin says then.

"It's too hot," I say.

"I might be able to get past it."

Catlin lays her hands on Lauren's head. She does something that puts out the flames. I try to follow, but the fire comes back up and I'm pushed back.

"You can't help," Catlin says. "Just wait. Call her name. That might help if I can bring her back part of the way."

So I call Lauren's name. I pace and call her name. I don't know how much time passes. Not a lot. Catlin steps away. She staggers, and I catch her, hold her up, while she gets her footing.

Lauren coughs and groans, but she wakes. Her eyes open. She looks at me.

"I heard you," she says to me.

"Unbelievable," I say, because what I think I've seen, what it feels like I've seen, is a miracle.

Catlin says. "Do you see me?"

She looks at her, nods. "My head feels like it's about to split open."

"She needs to stand," Catlin says to me.

I help lift Lauren up. She puts her arm over my shoulder. She staggers like she's drunk, like she can't get her legs to work right. Slowly she walks a little better.

"We need to take his ship," I say. "They'll be coming for us. They'll know."

Lauren still can't walk well so I help her to the ship.

I know, from the Reader, what to push to get the control to come out. The control is sort of like a DVD player; it slides out and that's where the driver's hand goes. That's how they connect. My hand is too big. "Stupid little aliens," I say.

Catlin frowns at me.

"I said aliens. Little aliens, not little people. Anyway," I go on, "you're going to have to drive."

Her hand fits fine. I tell her that it's interactive. Her mind controls it, but it also has to power it in certain ways. It's like a computer, but not.

"That's not really helpful."

"Sorry," I say.

I try to help her see what I've read. It's like seeing in a different way. Sort of like one of those paintings that looks like one thing, but if you stare at it long enough, it can look like something completely different. We have to see it differently to understand how to power the ship with our minds and to use the power it has. She fails to get it off the ground several times before it rises.

"Okay," she says. "Okay."

I tell her to go a little higher. The ships fly best thirty to forty feet off the ground.

"Turn west," I say.

She's confused by *west.* I say *left,* but that doesn't seem to help any. I point.

"I'm not good with directions," Catlin says.

That's an understatement, I think.

"I heard that," she says.

(((((**40**)))))

Catlin flies the ship pretty well. It wobbles every now and then, and once we unexplainably drop twenty feet, but mostly she's in control. We pass over the lake and see a whole line of transport ships off in the distance. As we get to the edge of town, we see a parking lot with thousands of little ships like ours parked in it.

We leave the city and we leave behind more dead. People just keep dying. When Anchise attacked the bus and almost killed me, for a brief second I felt something like relief. Finally, my turn. Finally, I wouldn't have to watch any more people I care about die. But I survived again. *It's just so hard sometimes.*

"It is hard," Catlin says, breaking into my thoughts.

"He was my best friend," I say.

"I'm sorry," Lauren says.

We lapse into silence. There's nothing more to say. We're all sorry.

We fly over a highway, into the sun, and do our best to keep going west. It gets much more difficult to be sure about our direction when the sun goes down. It gets more difficult to see the road, too, though the ship has headlights. Catlin is exhausted and falls asleep for a few seconds before I shake her awake. We're forced to land in a field. It's a bumpy landing, but no one gets hurt.

I feel a little safer here in the country. It's more familiar than the city, not so transformed by the aliens. There are stars in the sky, a familiar sky, and looking up, I can forget for a second what's happened to our world.

I'm sure they know about Anchise by now. Can they track us? I worry that we're too out in the open here. We passed a farmhouse a few miles back. I ask Catlin to fly us there. This turns out to be a bad idea. She gets the ship up just fine, but then we veer off course and into a line of trees. We crash right through the top of one. The ship's front caves in a little from the collision and something breaks. Catlin can't stop it then. We hit another tree and the front section of the ship is pushed to our knees. The shelf where Catlin has her hand retracts, and we have no control at all.

"Turn it off," Lauren shouts.

We hit a third tree, and this time the top of the

ship is torn off by branches. I shout, "Jump," which turns out to be completely unnecessary since both girls have already jumped.

The ship rises then, as if it was only waiting for the opportunity to get rid of its incompetent and dangerous pilot and crew. It floats up over the trees and heads back in the direction we came from. Its engine is making a sound like someone banging on a pot, but the sound gets farther and farther off. Then it's gone and all we hear is the silence.

We all agree that we should probably get some sleep, so we find a place under some trees.

The temperature has dropped since the sun went down, but we make beds out of leaves, and it's not so bad. It's not so good, either. We're cold and hungry, but exhaustion overcomes both, and after a while we all fall asleep. My sleep is deep and dreamless. I'm grateful for that.

It's funny how beautiful the sunrise is the next morning. The warmth on my face, the way the light falls across the field, all of it is so beautiful. In spite of everything, I'm grateful to be alive to see this, to feel something ninety-three million miles away warm my face.

Catlin and Lauren are still asleep. Catlin looks so young when she sleeps, like a kid. But we aren't young anymore. That's gone.

(((((41)))))

LORD VERTENOMOUS

Personal Log:

I sent Handlers after the three who killed Anchise and took his ship. It is beyond belief that primitives could kill him, but they did.

My wife annoys me with requests that I would normally be pleased to grant. This wilderness is harder on her than I'd imagined. My daughters miss their friends and school. Thinking of my family makes me angry. My plans have been ruined by product. It is intolerable. If my daughters and wife were not here, I would have followed the product myself and killed them. I would have betrayed the One and killed them slowly and rudely.

I checked on the Handlers. None of them

have training as trackers. They move slowly into the wilderness, finding and losing the runaway slaves' trail.

I'm at my desk, where there is much work to be done, but I don't do it. My father's last message burns in my mind. I have tried to destroy it, but he is powerful and communication from him, even from a great distance, is difficult to destroy.

I see it again and it fills me with anger.

Your last report is full of self-pity. You displease me. You should have seen the danger sooner and you should have taken immediate action. What have I taught you if not to always act quickly and decisively when confronted by a threat? Never wait for the other to strike first. Never think of losses. You hesitated out of greed. Do not complain to me of my scouts. Do not try to blame the company. This is your colony. You are the First Citizen. Any excuses only make your failure more evident. Destroy the runaways now. Contact me when you have succeeded.

This is my colony. So be it. I will make this colony work, and I will prove him wrong. I will do whatever I have to do to succeed. I will show him strength.

((((((42))))))

By afternoon, that warm, pleasant morning sun has become our enemy. It scorches us like it's scorched this brown, dusty earth. We turn various shades of red, Catlin the worst, a deep lobster color. Besides burning us and making us sweat, which allows dust to stick to every bare part of our skin, it dehydrates us. We've had no food or water since yesterday, and though the lack of food is uncomfortable, it's the thirst that really hurts. My throat is dry as sand, my lips crack painfully, and I'm unable to make even the tiniest drop of spit. I'm feeling pretty sorry for myself.

In spite of all this, Lauren keeps asking Catlin how she cured her. Her mouth is too dry to make words, so she uses her mind.

How did you know, though? How could you? she asks.

As though she's finally fed up, Catlin thinks, *I'm a freak, all right? It's lucky for you I am.*

I'm grateful, Lauren thinks. *I just don't understand how you'd know, how you could learn that fast. It's got to be like surgery or something.*

Lauren stops walking, and we all stop and stand uncertainly. It is a big, empty land, and it feels like we'll never get out of it.

But I have to admit that Lauren's questions aren't totally unreasonable. How could Catlin learn to do what she did? I mean, we've all learned things, but nothing like what she did for Lauren, nothing on that level. I've known from the start she was different but— and then I realize what I should have realized earlier.

You were like this, weren't you? I mean, before the invasion even. You were like we are now.

She looks surprised but tries to hide it with a shrug. *Not like this. I've increased in strength, too.*

Wait, Lauren thinks, *you're saying you had these abilities? Telepathic abilities?*

Weak ones.

How weak?

I couldn't talk to anyone with my mind yet. I could hear sometimes. I could do small things.

Lauren questions Catlin about what she could and

couldn't do. Now some of the things she was able to do before make sense.

My mom was a healer, she thinks. *I have her gift. She taught me a few things, but my formal training wouldn't have started until I graduated from high school.*

You brought me into your dream, didn't you? I think.

She shakes her head. *I made the connection. I could sometimes see other people's dreams. Yours were strong. But I could never do what you do. There are stories about dreamwalkers. Legends. No one I've known could dreamwalk.*

So you'd seen your mother do what you did for me? Lauren thinks, still trying to work out an explanation for what happened.

Not like that. My power has increased by being around them, too. I'm not even sure my mother could have done what I did. Like I said, we were very lucky.

But your whole family, Lauren thinks. *You all had these abilities?*

Some of us.

"We've got to keep moving," I say, though it doesn't seem like we've gotten anywhere all morning or that there is anyplace to get to. And I sure don't want to move again. But I take a step and another and another. The girls follow.

Lauren manages a few more questions, but after

a while we're all too hot, too burned, too sweaty, too thirsty, to do anything but mindlessly put one foot in front of the other.

We walk and we walk. Finally, in late afternoon Lauren spots a house. It's a big old ranch house that could use a coat of paint but that sits not far off the highway under a dozen shade trees. It looks like an oasis. We turn up the drive, and just being close to this place gives us energy.

"I see a well," I say.

"A shower," Lauren says. "There's got to be a shower."

"I want to drink my shower," I say.

"There's food," Catlin says.

"You can sense that there's food?" Lauren says.

"Power of positive thinking."

"Does that work?" Lauren says.

"I don't know."

"Oh, I thought, you know, it might be a talent or something."

"Uh, no. I think it's just some, like, lame psychology. My dad used to say it. Joke about it."

When we're almost to the door, Lauren says, "I don't know if I've thanked you properly for saving my life. Thank you."

Catlin says, "No problem."

We go inside.

There's water. We all drink and drink. It tastes unbe-
lievably good, in spite of a hint of metal in it. Lauren
goes and takes her shower.

There's electricity from somewhere; either it's still
being generated or the farm has a generator. I turn on
the window air conditioners. Catlin and I sit on the
sofa in the living room. It feels so good to sit. I could
fall asleep right there.

"Do you feel them more?" Catlin says.

"Who?" I say

"The rebels. It's like I feel them more, like they're
more real."

"I don't know," I say, but now that she says this, I
wonder if she could be right. They do seem more real.
I mean, I believe in them more. Could they be doing

it somehow? It's kind of a crazy thought, or at least it would have been a year ago.

Lauren comes out with a towel wrapped around her head. Her skin is brown, but there's a cute flush of red on her cheeks and across her nose. She looks clean and, I don't know, new somehow.

"You haven't checked out the food yet?" she says.

We shake our heads. She leads us into the kitchen.

Most of the food in the fridge is rotten. Some carrots are okay. We find a freezer in the garage though. Ice cream.

"Oh, how I've missed you," Lauren says, holding the carton to her cheek.

"What kind?" Catlin says.

"Chocolate chip," Lauren says.

"There is a God."

The girls go inside, but I want to look through the freezer. I find meat and some kind of frozen stew, which I bring in to show the girls.

"We've got this," Catlin says, holding up the ice cream. "Who cares?"

"Just in case we get tired of ice cream."

Lauren shakes her head at me. "You can't be serious. Maybe you didn't hear me. Chocolate chip, dude."

We get spoons and put the half gallon between us. We go at it, and it is better than I ever remember ice cream tasting.

I know it's unreasonable, but this house feels comfortable immediately, almost like a home. Maybe because the aliens aren't so near, I feel free in a way that I haven't in a long time, almost safe.

In a little family room off the kitchen, we find some DVDs. We decide on *The Fellowship of the Ring* and all sit on the sofa to watch.

Catlin says, "If we had some kick-ass heroes like those guys, no aliens would have ever conquered us. They wouldn't have had a chance."

"Aragorn," Lauren says, sighing and patting her heart. "I'm just saying, what couldn't the man do?"

"I know, right?" Catlin says. "The aliens would have just given up."

I could point out a few things. Like, for instance, Aragorn would have probably fallen asleep like most humans. He was just a man, after all. Now, Gandalf, maybe *he* could have helped. I keep quiet, though.

After a short while, Catlin falls asleep. Lauren and I finish the DVD. We're sitting on the sofa, Catlin sleeping right through everything, battle scenes and all. I ask Lauren if she has any brothers or sisters. Like me, she doesn't. This leads to talk about parents. Her parents were divorced.

"My dad ran off with his secretary. Talk about a cliché."

"You never saw him?"

"He left us. He didn't care about me. My mom remarried, and my stepdad was really cool. He's more like my real dad. Your parents weren't divorced, right?"

"No," I say. "They weren't."

"No one could make me crazy like my dad. I stole from him this one time my mom forced me to spend a weekend with him. I took all the money from his wallet, like a hundred dollars, and gave it to the first homeless person I could find." She blushes and shakes her head. "Crazy."

I put in the second DVD. It doesn't feel as comfortable in the room as it did. I don't realize until I sit back down how embarrassed she is. It's probably the only big thing she's ever done wrong.

"You were just mad," I say. "I got mad at my parents plenty of times."

"You never stole from them, I bet."

"Not from them. I did steal a car once and drive it into a lake."

"Why?"

"It was dumb. My wrestling coach moved me up two weights so his son could wrestle at my weight. He was a reserve behind me. The coach said he was doing it for the good of the team. That was a lie, though, because he could have just moved his son up. He weighed the same as I did."

"It's bad to be moved up?"

"I was wrestling someone about fifteen pounds heavier than me. It's a lot harder. That wasn't what made me mad, though. It was the way he did it. Lying like that. Using his power that way."

"So you stole his car."

"He loved that car. I shouldn't have taken it."

"We all do stupid things."

"The stupid thing was driving it into the lake. I got scared. I thought I was going to get caught, so instead of taking it back, I drove it into the lake. I don't regret taking the car so much as doing that."

We watch *The Two Towers* then. She leans into me and her head rests on my shoulder. She falls asleep. Then I fall asleep. I think it's the Ents, those huge, slow-moving, slow-talking trees, that finally make me unable to keep my eyes open.

I wake up. Catlin is shaking me.

"Someone is here," she whispers.

The TV is off. It's dark. I don't hear anything at first, but then I hear light footsteps.

"It's one of them," Catlin says.

(((((44)))))

We hold hands and join. I can join immediately with Catlin but it takes a few tries to get Lauren with us. I don't know how much stronger it makes us, but I know the aliens are confused and disturbed by our ability to do it. That's what I'm looking for, a second of confused and disturbed. An edge, however short-lived.

As I listen to him—not his footsteps, exactly, but his presence—I realize he's not a Handler. I can feel the difference. A Handler radiates power. We try to make ourselves invisible. The alien is feeling his way around, checking out the house. He senses someone, but he doesn't see us. His mind goes right past us.

He turns on lights in the kitchen. He knows someone has been here because of all the dishes in the sink, and I think he feels the memory of our presence, or something. But he's confused. No one could have been here recently.

We need his ship, I think.

I don't think he'll lend it to us, Catlin thinks.

Can we sneak by him? Lauren thinks.

He'll hear us. Maybe if we wait for him to fall asleep, we can get by him.

His mind is in the room. He's standing in the kitchen, but I hear his mind in here, listening to us. I run toward the doorway. I don't know if he's going to run or if he's trying to block us so that we can't.

Lauren and Catlin are right behind me. He looks at the three of us. He's confused but not frightened. He seems almost excited.

"You're human?" he says, his voice, like all of theirs, strained by speaking out loud.

"Don't move," I say, like I've got him covered.

"Right," he says. "You've got me covered. I've seen some of your movies. Very good." Then he looks at Catlin. "Very small for a human, aren't you? Are you a midget? No, wait, dwarf. One is proportionate to the larger of your species and one is not. I believe it's dwarves that aren't proportionate."

"I'm neither," Catlin says indignantly. "I'm a girl. I'm just small. Anyway, we call them little people."

He smiles and nods appreciatively. "Yes, yes. Little

people. That's very good. I certainly intend to call them little people if I ever come across any."

He looks each of us over; he seems pleased.

"All human?" he says, nodding. "What a welcome surprise."

"Yes, we're all human." I can tell that Lauren is irritated by his enthusiasm.

"A surprise and an honor. I was looking forward to meeting humans, but I never anticipated meeting humans in the wild, the natural habitat, shall we say?"

He takes a step toward us, and we all instinctively move back.

"I'm not going to harm you," he says. Then he frowns and shakes a finger at us. "Unless of course you attack me. I'm aware of the violent streak in your species."

I'm angry that I jumped back. I can hear in the tone of his voice that he thinks he's in control. Like the other aliens, he thinks we're weak.

"Stay over there," I order.

"I suppose you three hid somehow when the first forces came through and have managed to evade the patrols. There'll be a lot more of them now with the second landing."

"We didn't—"

Lauren interrupts me. "Didn't get caught because we are clever enough to stay out of their way."

I realize she's right. No need for him to know the truth about us.

He goes on, oblivious to Lauren's lie. "I've never seen a conquering. I know they can be quite brutal, though. I'm sorry for your losses. What are your names? I do love human names. So short. So simple. There is much to admire about your species."

"Who are you?" I say. I mean *Who are you?* as in *What are you doing here?* and *Why do you act so differently from the other aliens we've met?* but he takes it as an invitation to introduce himself.

"I'm Bartemous Mortarellius the fourth."

I say, "Okay, Bart, but what I mean is, why are you here, out here, away from the others?"

"Bart?" he says, chuckling. "That is good. Bart. Yes, thank you. Call me Bart. The beginning of one of your famous novels, I believe. 'Call me Ishmael.' *Moby-Duck.*"

"*Moby-Dick,*" I say.

"Are you sure?"

I can tell he's disappointed that he got the name wrong.

"I've never read it," I say, "but ducks are little birds that float on lakes. They aren't great white whales."

Lauren interrupts. "Why are you here?"

He tries to push his mind into hers. He wants to

know why she's curious. I hear this. That's his thought, like he's studying her or something.

"Ouch," he says when she shoves him out. "How did you do that?"

"I didn't ask you in," she says. "You were being rude."

"But you can't do that." He looks from Catlin to me to Lauren. "Product can't—humans can't—do that. I'm an expert. I've studied you for a long time."

"I guess you're not a very good expert, then," Lauren says.

"I am the best," he says, obviously hurt. Then he becomes indignant. "I am considered the foremost authority. It is why I was allowed on the second landing."

He eyes us more closely. He says, "You look like humans, but perhaps you are not humans." His guard goes up. I feel the way his mind puts up some kind of shield and how he forces himself to be more alert.

He doesn't seem like the others, Catlin thinks to me.

He's an alien, I think.

But not like the others we've met, she thinks.

"You're communicating?" Bart says. "You cannot be communicating. Come now, what species are you? How did you get here? I really am quite cross with you. I thought I was meeting authentic humans."

"We're humans," I say.

"Something is quite wrong here. I have studied humans for a very long time."

"So you're one of the scouts," Catlin says.

"Goodness, no," he says. "I've nothing to do with the military. I'm a scholar, a teacher in the esteemed—oh, never mind, in one of our great universities. I have been studying your culture ever since we first noticed your planet. I've taught several sections on you."

"We're human," I say. "I guess you don't know as much about us as you think."

He sits down on the sofa, looking perplexed and thoughtful. He pulls a handkerchief out of his pocket and wipes his large forehead. He says, "It is quite hot out here. Brown and hot. Not at all like the brochures promise. Of course I was aware of deserts. I simply didn't expect them to be so large and empty. You really are humans?"

Really, Lauren thinks. *Two females. One male. Able to hear. Not product. You've all made a mistake.*

He tries to force his way into our thoughts again. He gets something from Lauren, though she tries to shove him out again. Catlin and I block him. He sighs sort of dramatically. He is heavier than the Handlers, heavier even than Addyen's husband, and there's something almost playful in those big, round eyes of his.

"No need to be coy with me," he says. "I'm a scholar, not a government official. You couldn't hear before we came, could you?"

"No," I say, cautiously. He may not be like the other aliens, but he's still an alien. I don't want him to know about Catlin or her family.

He nods. "As I thought. There is precedent. A species with brains capable of connecting to the One, yet unable to do so until they were stimulated by contact with us. It caused quite a stir. Yes, it did. Many, many citizens of the Republic were deeply disturbed by the destruction and enslavement of a species with latent powers. For a time, all colonization was suspended. But no further cases were discovered in other colonies and, of course, the need for settlements eventually overcame conscience. I think your species is quite familiar with that compromise, even in your short history."

I decide I should tell him we're runaways. If he knows, then he'll be in the same position as Addyen. He'll have to let everyone know we're not product. I'm about to tell him when Catlin blurts out, "We're runaways. We weren't overlooked—we escaped."

She's about to go on. I want her to, and I can tell Lauren does, too. It's like we need to tell him, someone, anyone.

"No more," he says. "Best you keep this to yourselves."

"You need to know," I say. "You need to know how they killed everyone at his house and what they did to a Sanginian who tried to help us."

"We need your help," Catlin says.

"It would be a very bad idea. I'm a scholar. Cowardly when it comes to the ways of the world. I live in what you call the ivory tower, which, by the way, is not at all true. Academics live in houses just like everyone else. Another one of your metaphors, I suppose. They're quite misleading. At any rate, I certainly can't help you. Better save your stories for a more appropriate audience, someone who can act with vigor and courage."

"You're already helping runaways," I say. "Lord Vert would kill you for that. What do you have to lose?"

"Lord Vert?" he says, smiling. "That is a good name. You are certainly very creative with names." But then his smile dies as he looks nervously around the room. "Of course, you should call him by his proper name and you should not involve me. How could I have known that you're runaways? I've been in the field since I landed. No, I'm completely ignorant."

"You're a scholar," Lauren says. "You should hear

what's happened to us. You should learn what you can from a primary source."

He's silent and then he sighs with what I think of as a fat man's sigh, sort of puffy, and leans back into the hard sofa. "I suppose, for purely historical reasons I should hear what you have to say."

"But you won't be ignorant if you do," I say.

He makes a sound that is a lot like a *humph*.

"Please," Lauren says.

"Fine," he says. "Tell me."

Bart, it turns out, does not have a ship. Just our luck, he's some kind of alien anthropologist who left his ship behind to discover America or something. He's driving a 1976 Chevy truck—1976! Ancient. He thinks driving an old piece of junk is going to get him in touch with our culture. I ask him how he thought driving an old truck could help him understand us more than driving a nice new sports car?

"I want to feel what the average American feels," Bart says.

"You think the average American drives a truck over thirty years old?"

"America is my specialty," he says, like I'm supposed to bow before his expertise.

"I am an American," I remind him, though I guess it would be more accurate to say *was* now.

He makes a little sound. I think it might be another alien *humph.* He's driving us down the lonely highway. The windows are open because the old piece-of-junk truck doesn't even have air conditioning. Luckily, Bart has supplies, including water, stored in a special container, like a cooler except that it stays cool without ice. We're going in the general direction of Taos, which is not the same thing as taking the right road, but it's the best we can do without maps.

Bart keeps asking questions. He wants to know about TV, which I use as an opportunity to give him my views on lame reality shows. He's also big on sports, especially football. When I bring up wrestling, he has no knowledge of it, which is irritating. I can hear Michael laughing and saying, "See, Tex, even aliens know about football." I miss him.

Bart tells us a little about his trip here, which took years. Apparently they live a lot longer than we do.

"I stopped at Remus, a planet where I plan to spend my declining years. It is a lovely place that holds the older male in high regard. The female species, in fact, considers the elder male far more attractive than the younger. I always enjoy my stays."

"Sounds like the young females get a bad deal," Lauren says.

"They do not think so," he says.

Lauren asks him some questions about the aliens'

history and this leads to an argument about slavery. She points out that no civilized society can have slaves.

"I believe yours did," he reminds her.

"Not for a long time. How can you? I mean, when you're so advanced, how can you justify slavery?"

He seems to ponder the question. He says, "It's considered necessary. We have a drive to expand. It is a biological necessity. We need slaves for the physical work of expansion. And there are many in our world who claim slavery is good for primitives. It brings them into the larger universe. We are able to show them the ways of the One. They become part of our Republic and civilization and sometimes, after several generations, they earn their freedom. The truth is, there are worse conquering species in the universe. The machine worlds destroy those they conquer. There are many justifications, but there are also many who oppose slavery. Personally, I am against it. If you entertain notions of harming me, I think you should remember that."

It's a good thing he's against it, though I'm not entirely convinced. But a bad thing for us is that he is a very poor driver. He keeps driving on the shoulder. I remind him that it's not considered part of the road, which he finds difficult to accept.

"Is it not of the same substance?"

"Yes."

"Is it not the same color?"

"Just stay on the road."

"But it certainly seems connected to the road. How am I to distinguish road from nonroad when you seem incapable of identifying their differences?"

The day warms up as the morning turns into afternoon. It quickly becomes a copy of yesterday. The sun smolders in an endlessly blue sky and beats the brown, cracked earth into submission.

Bart wants to know why we want to go to New Mexico. "Texas is a much more significant state," he points out. "It was here that the glorious Texans fought to death in the famous battle of the Alamo. Davy Crockett was most famous for his final stand and his cat-skin cap. He was a great hero. He lives on forever in the heart of every American, this hero. Your greatest actor, John Wayne, played him in a movie."

"He wasn't our greatest actor," I say.

"Partner. He was always calling everyone 'partner' in his movies. I did not understand that."

"And no one ever wore a cat-skin hat," Lauren says.

They argue about this for a while. Just to stir things up I mention that there was a book about a cat in a hat, which earns me a scornful glance from Lauren and a perplexed one from Bart.

"Anyway," he finally says, as if he is not exactly caving but wants to move on, "why go to New Mexico?"

"Far away from everything," I say. "Not very green."

I'm careful to hide my thoughts of rebels, though every time I think of Taos, I think of them.

"Ah," he says. "Right. The rock formations."

"Yes."

"Ah," he says. "I see. You believe it is safer because of our reduced abilities."

"Reduced abilities?" Lauren says.

He nods. "Oh, yes. Higher altitudes slightly weaken our abilities. Handlers are less affected, of course."

"You don't like the Handlers much, do you?" Catlin says.

"I'm an old man, but I have a high regard for life, particularly my own. Handlers are bringers of death. They're warriors. After an invasion and a year or two of settlement, most of them will find another invasion force to join. A few will settle on a planet, though, and inevitably they bring death to those around them, citizens and noncitizens alike."

We come to a strange reddish land that drops away from us on both sides. It's as if we're in the mountains here, except that we haven't gone up; the land has dropped off around us.

"Remarkable," Bart says. "It reminds me of a

Rantanpull moon. A little more green and it would be quite beautiful here."

He's about to say more when we see it in the sky in front of us, hovering just above the road: a ship.

"Let us hope this is a patrol and not a Handler," Bart says calmly. For a coward, he's pretty cool.

(((((46)))))

I grab Lauren's and Catlin's hands, and we make ourselves invisible. It's getting a little easier each time we do it.

"Remarkable," Bart says. "Absolutely remarkable. Only the strongest among us are capable of joining. Handlers, whose strength is like those of your knights in the Middle Ages, lords, generals—only a few besides these can join. It is remarkable. Your joining is primitive and crude, but the fact that you can do it at all is truly remarkable."

I hear Catlin think that the alien reminds her of her dad. She thinks it's strange and kind of funny.

Bart pulls the truck over to the side of the road, and the engine sputters, then dies. The ship lands right in the center of the road.

Bart gets out of the truck and walks toward the ship. We can feel that the alien in the ship is not a Handler, which is good news. He looks Bartemous over carefully, and when he's satisfied he's not a threat, he walks toward him. They meet about fifteen feet away from us.

The patrol asks Bartemous questions about what he is doing and why and tells him to be on the lookout for runaways. Bartemous raises one thin eyebrow (I have noticed that this is the one place they seem to have hair, these faint half-moons over their eyes). The patrol tells him that the rumors of product escaping from Lord Vertenomous are true.

He has made them runaways. We are all on alert.

Troubling, Bart replies.

The patrol nods in agreement. *Be careful. Check in at the stations to make sure you aren't in violation. I'm told this area will be cordoned off soon. They're going to reform it.*

Bartemous thanks him. He comes back to the truck as the ship takes off.

"What did he mean, *reform?*" I ask Bart after the patrol ship is out of sight.

"This land is not suitable for settlement. They have reformers who will plant and cultivate and work on making areas more suitable to us. It will never be preferred land, but we like to use as much of a planet as possible. Even the worst land is used for training soldiers, penal colonies, or places to store what cannot be reused."

The land on both sides of the road drops away more steeply and creates deeper and wider valleys. Catlin spots a farm down at the bottom of one of the canyons with a stream running past it. Since it's almost dark, we agree that it would be a good place to rest. It's a good decision; the farmhouse is in excellent shape and we're low on water.

Once we settle in, Bartemous offers to cook dinner. He goes to the kitchen to make something from whatever he can find that isn't spoiled.

"He'll find us," Catlin says, her face looking pale. "Lord Vertenomous. He'll find us."

"He won't," I say.

"We're hundreds of miles away from him now," Lauren says.

I say, "We shouldn't tell Bart about the rebels."

Everyone agrees.

"When we find them, we'll be safe," Lauren says.

"Safer," I say. I can't help correcting her. We won't ever be safe.

"They're out there," Catlin says. "I'm even more sure of it now."

"Are they sending out some kind of signal?" Lauren says. "Could they be? Because I feel the same way. More sure."

It feels stronger to me, too, though I realize we might be feeling that way because we want to. I'm tempted to tell them about my dream about Taos, but I feel foolish. Anyway, I don't want to say something that might upset them; it was only a dream.

"Tell us more about your family," Lauren says to Catlin.

"Only my mom's side of the family had talents."

"What kind of talents?"

"Different people in the family had different talents. It's like how some people can play music or write or are good at math or sports. My mother once healed a bullet wound in my father so that he was better in twenty minutes."

I don't ask why her father had a bullet wound, though I'm curious. I ask what other talents people had.

"Some of my cousins could predict the weather and even sometimes cause it to rain. My uncle was strong enough that he could cause a stinging sensation in another person's feet that made it difficult for them to walk. He could also move small objects, like a fork or a spoon on a table. My mother always said he was foolish, though, because he showed off. He would show people his abilities, people not of our clan. My mother was always scolding him but she couldn't get him to stop."

I understand her mom's concern. People with our kind of abilities wouldn't have been welcomed by the world. Back in the day, they would have been considered tools of the devil. But even today, before the invasion, I mean, people would have been afraid of these powers. Of us.

"What do you mean by *clan?*" Lauren says

"Most people with talents belong to clans, old clans. They're small. Ours was, anyway. There are a few outsiders who have no clan, but I don't know much about them."

Bartemous steps into the room and says dinner is ready. I jump up like I can't wait to eat, but I really just want to hide our conversation. The alien may be a friend, but he's still an alien. We can't depend on the kindness of aliens.

At dinner he talks about machines. He wants to know how we came to rely on them so much. None of us have very good answers. They make life easier is about all we can say.

"That's the general consensus around the universe," Bart says. "They make life easier until they don't. One day the machines wake up and look around and realize they're doing all the work. On that day, they decide a change is in order."

We're all picking at our food. Clearly, not all aliens have the cooking gene. This is nothing like Addyen's food. Bart mixed canned vegetables together and then put in canned mixed fruit with the juice. He found some frozen steaks but he didn't thaw the meat. He just cooked it. It's still frozen in the middle.

"You didn't save us," I say.

"No, but that day was coming. You would not have escaped that day."

((((47))))

I don't sleep much that night. The exhaustion that made me sleep soundly the night before is gone, replaced by a nervous energy. I get up before sunrise and walk out onto the red earth, climbing around the big rocks as the sky lightens. I find a spot among the rocks and watch the sky and earth turn the same color and then separate. It's here that Catlin finds me. She sits beside me on my ledge. For a while she doesn't say anything, just watches the sunrise with me.

"Maybe we should just stay here," she says after a while. "Life wouldn't be so bad here, would it?"

"We'd probably survive longer."

Her face darkens.

"I'm sorry," I say.

The long shadows of the hills are shortening, and the cutting cold of the night weakens as the sun shines on us. It's a perfect morning. But I know this perfect morning will turn into another scorching day before it's even noon.

I see Lauren step out of the house onto the front porch. She squints into the sun and raises her arm to block it. She reminds me of a line from a song I heard a long time ago in the car, on an oldies station my mom liked. It was kind of dumb. It was something like, "I'd go through the darkest night to see the way you look when the morning sun hits your eyes." Dumb. Still something about the way she looks reminds me of that line. I wave my arm and shout her name so she knows where we are and that we're all right. She waves back and goes inside.

"We won't ever be safe, will we?" Catlin says.

I could lie, but I don't. "No."

"I don't want to die. I did for a while when he had me locked in that tower. I planned on finding a way to kill myself."

"What stopped you?"

She looks up at me with her very green eyes. "You did. You came into my room, and I wasn't alone."

"We aren't going to die," I say.

We stay a little longer, and then we make our way back down the rocks. By the time we reach the house, the sun is pushing up into the sky and I'm already starting to sweat.

(((((48)))))

LORD VERTENOMOUS

Personal Log:

One of the patrol has called with news. He's spotted the runaways. He's read one of the females and knows they are traveling to a town once called Taos. He gave me the coordinates and asked if he should send patrols. I told him no. I will take care of this.

I've told Adamanous, my strongest Handler, to ready two ships. He asked if I wanted patrol to meet us there. I let him see my scorn. Am I not Lord Vertenomous, son of a senator, descendant of those who have been part of the ruling class for generations? Do I not have strength enough to kill runaway slaves? If we are lucky enough to run into the troublesome rebels, do I not have strength enough to kill them with a wave of my hand?

We do not need patrol, I told him coldly. *We will put an end to this today.*

I'm in the room where I kept the girl. I would tear her apart if she were here now, but I feel an unpardonable nostalgia for those nights we lay in bed before the other colonists arrived. Of course it is not the slave girl that I miss. It is those nights when success and an increase to my reputation seemed certain. It is not my fault. But I admit something here that I will only allow myself to admit now and only once. I knew that girl had more power than someone with no link to the One. I knew she was not product. I should have killed her immediately.

It is a secret I will bury deep.

We drive west, and before long we're out of the red canyons and the land flattens around us. We come to Lubbock, where we find a grocery store.

We have to force the sliding doors open because the electricity is off here. The smell is pretty awful: spoiled milk and rotten fruit, vegetables, and meat. The store is dim without lights, but I can see well enough to tell that the shelves have plenty of food on them. We find the water bottles right away and each grab one and slug it down, even Bart.

Bart says he's thrilled to be in a food storage unit, but that he imagined it would be larger.

"I would like to find the cereal that the great champions of your games ate," he says.

Blank stares. We're all a little dazed with heat and travel, but I doubt any of us would have known what he was talking about even if we were alert.

"Wheaties, breakfast of champions," he says.

Right.

Lauren suggests we get carts and load up; we have the truck, after all, and who knows when we'll get another chance to shop. She and I take a cart to one side of the store and Catlin and Bart head toward the other. As they walk off, I hear Catlin breaking the news to Bart that anyone could eat the "breakfast of champions."

It's kind of strange to be pushing a cart through the dim, abandoned grocery store. Lauren says she's always liked shopping. She finds it relaxing.

"Of course I could do without the smell."

"You did this for fun, didn't you?" I say.

"Maybe," she says.

We're at the granola section and she really goes crazy. She loads up. Surprise, surprise. Once the cart is weighted down with bags of granola and granola bars and granola thingies, we push on to the chips section. She has the nerve to complain when I put some chips in the cart because she says they're empty calories.

"Listen, granola girl, maybe I want some empty calories. Maybe I need something to offset all that roughage or whatever I'm going to get from granola."

"You might as well eat grass," she says.

"I don't like grass. I do like potato chips."

"Grass has about as much to do with a potato as those chips you've got."

Another aisle over we're in the chocolate section, and not surprisingly, given that she's a girl, she puts some chocolate in the cart. I point out that she's adding to our empty calorie collection, but she claims studies have shown that chocolate fights cancer. She actually cites one of the studies.

We brush against each other a lot as we load up the cart. It's like a little shock each time we do, a pleasant shock. Finally I kiss her. I just do it. She kisses me back. She feels soft and I'm lost in that softness. My arms are around her, my hands on her back. I feel her body press against mine. So there we are making out in the stale air and rotting food smell of the grocery store at the end of the world.

"Romantic," she says finally.

"Well, I wanted to wait for just the right moment."

Catlin and Bart push their cart around the corner and into our aisle. Bart says, "We'd better get going."

Catlin looks from Lauren to me and smiles. "Shopping can be fun, can't it?"

"We must go," Bart says.

"Hope there's not a line," I say.

"Gallows humor," Lauren says, but smiles.

We go through checkout and I say, "Guy says everything is free today. It's a free day."

"To whom is he speaking?" Bart asks Catlin.

"No one," she says. "He's just in a good mood all of a sudden. I wonder why."

"Were there free days? Days when all food was free?"

"Never," she says.

He looks annoyed and seems about to ask another question but decides against it. We load the groceries into bags and cart them out to the truck. One of the bags splits open as I lift it in.

"*Intercourse!*" I shout. "*Supreme Being condemn it to the fires of hell.*"

Bart may be an alien, but the way he's looking at me is familiar: perplexed and a little troubled. Catlin and Lauren laugh.

"This does not seem like normal human behavior," Bart says in that professorial voice he uses sometimes.

"It is," I say.

"No, it's not," both the girls say at the same time, which just sets them off on another laughing jag.

I offer Lauren the window seat because she's been sitting in the middle and looking kind of miserable there. She says I'd be really uncomfortable in the middle. There's not enough room. Catlin suggests Lauren sit on my lap, then smiles innocently. Lauren and I discuss the possibility for a while, each coming up with reasons for and against it, and I catch Catlin rolling her eyes. I finally ask Lauren if she would please just sit there.

"That's my gun," I say when she shifts away from my lap like she's sat on a tack. I just want to be clear, but I guess I've said it kind of abruptly.

Both Lauren and I turn red.

"Embarrassment," Bartemous says with way too much enthusiasm. "Blood rushing to the face. I've read about it."

We find the interstate. I consider messing with Bart some more by talking about how light the traffic is, but I don't because I'm suddenly aware of how empty everything feels. A city without people is unnatural. The loneliness of it is all around me, like air, and, like air, I have to breathe it in. I have no choice.

We're into the mountains by midafternoon, and by evening we've reached Taos.

(((((50)))))

Just after we cross the gorge, I hear others like us, or at least one other human mind. I'm sure of it. Then, as we get into town, it's gone. Something else is present, something large and powerful and definitely not human.

"We made it," Lauren says, sounding surprised and happy. She doesn't hear what's going on, so she doesn't know that we've made it right into a trap.

"This is very bad," Bartemous says.

We turn off the main street and into a plaza, the plaza of my dream. Bartemous is concentrating on putting up a shield. Something smashes it to pieces like it's nothing; Bart groans and slumps over the wheel. A second later the truck crashes against a wall I can't see. I'm thrown forward into the windshield.

Something sharp cuts into my forehead and blood trickles down my cheek. The doors of the truck fly off their hinges and I'm yanked out; we all are. No one physically touches us, but it feels like giant hands are reaching out and batting us around.

Then there's wind behind us, and it blows me—all of us—across the plaza. My knees and my elbows scrape against the pavement as I tumble over it. Skin rips from my hands as I try to break my fall and grab for anything I can. I get hold of a small tree in a planter, but it snaps as I'm shoved on by the wind.

Bart wakes up enough to mumble, "I am a citizen of the Republic."

He tries to say it louder, but the wind eats up his words. Then the wind dies as quickly as it came, and I'm still. Something holds me to the ground. It's holding the others, too, including Bart. Then I see Lord Vert. It's the first time I've seen his physical self. He's larger than even the Handler next to him. His skin has a deeper green.

These killed a Handler. He turns to the Handler beside him. *Hard to believe. Slaves. Look at them.*

The Handler seems almost embarrassed by something, but he looks at us.

I am a citizen, Bart thinks with as much authority as someone whose face is pushed into the pavement can have. More than I would have thought. *I am a man of reputation, a scholar. You must release me immediately.*

A scholar? Lord Vertenomous replies. *Surely a scholar knows the penalty for assisting runaways. I am Lord Vertenomous, scholar. You dare to tell me what I must do?*

I was not—

I feel Lord Vertenomous's mind move, and Bart goes silent. We're all lifted to our feet and then off the ground. It's then that I realize Bart is dead.

Sorry for your loss, Lord Vertenomous thinks. He turns to us then, but he avoids looking at Catlin. She looks right at him. *Now, where are the others?*

I feel Lord Vertenomous pushing into me, and I throw up a door and slam it shut. He's surprised. He bangs on it. I manage to keep it shut, though I feel it give, feel that in a second it will break apart. Before it does, the Handler distracts him.

This one—the Handler points to Lauren—*came here to find them. They came because they believed the rebels are here, but they know nothing.*

Lord Vertenomous looks angry then. *Disgusting creatures. Look at them.*

Then I feel his anger turn to me, feel it like something smothering me, like hands around my throat. I gasp for breath. I hear Catlin rush at him with her mind, but he pushes her away like she's made of paper. Lauren is being held by the Handler.

My breath is gone. I'm losing consciousness. When I'm just to the edge, I'm pulled back. I drop to the ground. I hear the others hit the ground, too. I look up and see Lord Vertenomous looking around the square. I feel his surprise.

People come out of the small shops all around us, probably fifty or sixty of them. I can hear their minds. Some of them join in the imperfect and messy way that Lauren and Catlin and I join. I feel the power of those joined increase. There are ten in one group. The others have fewer. Even that group of ten is still not as strong as the Handler and certainly not as strong as Lord Vertenomous, but there are so many attackers that some of them get past the Handler's defenses and he falls, overpowered. They've killed him. They've killed him *with their minds*.

I get to my feet. The impossible *is* possible. Lord Vertenomous is fighting the rebels. A ring of energy expands out from him and breaks against them, and a lot of them fall. I throw something like a roundhouse kick. He turns to block it and slips slightly. I see it then, an open place, a chance. I throw everything I've got at Lord Vertenomous. I hit him with my mind, my heart, everything that makes me human.

The wind comes back and I'm blown onto my butt and I think I've missed. Then I feel the wind reverse back into him. It makes a sucking sound, and branches break from trees and everything is pulled toward Lord Vertenomous. But all this lasts only a second.

He's dead.

I look around the square. I stand up slowly, and I see the people. They don't look like a commercial for Target, that's for sure. They look dirty, and their clothes are worn, and they're beaten up. There are many lying on the ground; some are dead, and some of them are alive but hurt. Catlin goes to help whomever she can. I hear people say, "Healer." Lauren comes to my side.

"You killed him," a woman says. "The alien, the strong one. You fought the same way they fight."

"I don't know," I say. I'm confused by what she says. I'm in shock and I hurt all over.

Others are whispering the same thing. *He fought like they fight. He killed the alien that called himself a lord.*

The crowd parts as two men walk up to us. One has long white hair and the other is blond. They look like father and son. The younger one is my age or a little older.

"You led them here," the one about my age says accusingly.

"We didn't know they were following us," Lauren says.

The people around are quiet now, waiting for the man with white hair to speak. He's their leader, obviously. There's something about him that feels young and strong even though he looks old. "You kill like they kill. How did you learn to kill that way?"

"I don't know," I say.

"He is a warrior," one of the women says.

Someone else whispers the word.

The blond guy swings around and glares at the woman who spoke. "That doesn't make him a warrior. One kill doesn't make him a warrior."

"You had this power before the aliens invaded?" The white-haired man asks me. "The power of a warrior?"

"No."

"No," he says, as if he is agreeing with me.

"He doesn't know anything," the guy my age says. "He was lucky. The alien was being attacked on all sides and he was lucky."

"No," White Hair says. "No one has that much luck."

"We need to go," the young guy says. "More will be coming."

"Do you wish to come with us?" White Hair says to me and Lauren.

"They were tracking them," the young guy says. "That's one of their lords dead there. The aliens will come looking for these three, and we'll be in even more danger."

"She is not a new blood," White Hair says pointing at Catlin, who is bent over an injured person. "She is a healer. And he kills like they kill. They will add to our strength. In any event, we cannot leave them."

I look at Lauren. She nods.

"We'll come," I say.

"I am Lorenzo Sergio de Cabeza the third, but you may call me Doc."

"You're a doctor?" Lauren says.

"Not the medical kind. Two PhDs. I was an indecisive youth."

The younger guy stomps off, but everyone else seems happy to have us. Many of them welcome us. Doc tells us to jump into one of the truck beds. We do. Our truck joins a convoy of trucks and jeeps heading up into the mountains.

One of the three boys sitting in our truck says, "Welcome to New America."

"New America?" I say "Where's New America?"

"We're New America," he says. "That's what Doc calls us."

New America. All the death. All we've lost. It seems like too much. How can there be a New America?

Then Lauren takes my hand. Her hand is small and smooth.

"New America," she says like she's deciding something.

I look at Lauren and at the trees and at the blue sky, and I take my world back. It's our world. Ours.

Acknowledgments

I want to thank my wife, Frances Hill, for her patience and encouragement. Thanks to my agent, Sara Crowe, for her persistent faith and encouragement and, of course, finding a home for my work. Thanks to all the staff at Candlewick, particularly my editor, Jennifer Yoon, for insightful edits, thoughtful suggestions, and plain hard work on this manuscript. Thanks also to my writing group: Varian Johnson, April Lurie, Julie Lake, Frances Hill, and Helen Hemphill. Also thanks to my one-day writing group: Don Tate, Debbie Gonzales, Shana Burg, and Donna Bowman Bratton. Last, thanks to my parents, Bill and Agnes Yansky, for their ridiculous assertion that my sister and I could be whatever we wanted to be. Sometimes ridiculous assertions can make all the difference.